MISSION CONTAMINATION

Across The UK

Edited By Allie Jones

First published in Great Britain in 2019 by:

Young Writers
Remus House
Coltsfoot Drive
Peterborough
PE2 9BF
Telephone: 01733 890066
Website: www.youngwriters.co.uk

FOREWORD

Young Writers was created in 1991 with the express purpose of promoting and encouraging creative writing. Each competition we create is tailored to the relevant age group, hopefully giving each student the inspiration and incentive to create their own piece of work, whether it's a poem, mini saga or a short story. We truly believe that seeing their work in print gives students a sense of achievement and pride in their work and themselves.

Our Survival Sagas series aimed to challenge both the young writers' creativity and their survival skills! One of the biggest challenges, aside from dodging diseased hordes and avoiding the contagion, was to create a story with a beginning, middle and end in just 100 words!

Inspired by the theme of contamination, whether from a natural mutation, a chemical attack or a man-made experiment gone wrong, their mission was to craft tales of fear and redemption, new beginnings and struggles of survival against the odds. As you will discover, these students rose to the challenge magnificently and we can declare *Mission Contamination* a success.

The mini sagas in this collection are sure to set your pulses racing and leave you wondering with each turn of the page: are these writers born survivors?

CONTENTS

Aimee Patricia Walker (16) 66
Jodie Shaw (16) 67
Ben Rees 68
Dylan Franklin (16) 69
Jonas Benjamin Barnley (12) 70
Callum James Close (13) 71
Carla Brown (12) 72

Coleraine Grammar School, Coleraine

Kyle Jackson 73
Clara Macy McNicholl (12) 74
Thomas Brown (13) 75
Jack Embleton (13) 76

Craigavon Senior High School, Lurgan

Madison Ogle (15) 77
Weronika Mroz (15) 78

Crumlin Integrated College, Crumlin

Cara Calvin (14) 79
Taylir Costello (12) 80
Lucy Elliott (12) 81
Ella Falloon (11) 82

Five Islands Academy, St Marys

Kenny Gibson (12) 83
Emily Hobbs (11) 84
Ava Elizabeth Joan Kearsley (11) 85
Hafwen Bryher Kendrick (11) 86

Groomsport Intensive Support Unit, Groomsport

James Church 87

Haileybury Turnford School, Cheshunt

Henry Wayne Gibbons (13) 88
Mackenzie Warren (12) 89
Lelde Voita (12) 90
Kirsty Dewberry (15) 91
Mackenzie Paulding (12) 92
Amy Richardson (14) 93
Courtney Cioffi (15) 94
Toby Sharples (13) 95
Lewis Butteriss 96
Billy Fairclough (12) 97
Aimee Jordan (13) 98
Ruby Lincoln (11) 99
Tom Garcia (12) 100
Flavius Ionut Ghita (15) 101
Kitty Elizabeth Piper (13) 102
Isaac Shallow (14) 103
Ellie Newman (13) 104
Alexander Alderson (12) 105
Lily Clayton (11) 106
Bruno Hascec (13) 107
Heyden Sookaree (13) 108
Pelayia Panayides (13) 109

Hazelwood College, Newtownabbey

Jose Noah Sollano Monghit (13) 110
Caoimhghin McAtamney (12) 111

Hockerill Anglo-European College, Bishop's Stortford

Sara Ipakchi (16) 112

Loreto College, Coleraine

Sophie Crawford (14) 113
Grace McConnell (14) 114

Penrice Academy, St Austell

Leo Carmichael (12)   115

St Christopher School, Letchworth Garden City

Jack Chimes (14)   116
Poppy Holden-Adams (14)   117
Archie Holt (13)   118
William McGinley (11)   119
Johnny Haase (14)   120

St George Catholic College, Swaythling

Louis Manchip (13)   121
Olivia Redmond (12)   122
Katie Hunter (11)   123
Toni Euler-Ajayi   124
Joash Siby (12)   125
Dawid Kwiecien (13)   126
Isobel Linda Louise Moran (12)   127
Ruben Luca Blaise Aburrow (12)   128
Evan Jay Sayas (12)   129
Reuben McDermott (12)   130
Maksymilian Slonka (13)   131
Bronwyn Springett (12)   132
Pablo Tombaccini-Maestro (12)   133
Gabby Markelyte (11)   134
Raphael Garcia (12)   135
Nevin Biju Joseph (13)   136
Oscar Sadler-Abert (12)   137
Joe Oliver Stockley (12)   138
Leo Thompson (11)   139
Zaina Anwar (11)   140
Caleb Fairman (12)   141
Claudio Araujo (12)   142
Chloe Longfellow (11)   143
Grace Lily Robins (12)   144
Bethany Quester (12)   145
Toby Lucas   146
Lydia McLoughlin-Parker (11)   147
Matthew Hamblyn (12)   148

Danial Khan (12)   149
Edward Rayner (12)   150
Charles Hiscock (12)   151
Joshua Spradbery (12)   152

St Killian's College, Carnlough

Ann Esme McAuley (13)   153
Maggi McKillion (14)   154
Nikola Lawniczak (15)   155
Tara Leopold (12)   156
Cara McAuley (13)   157
Ellie-Jo Butler (13)   158
Peter McAuley (12)   159
Theo McToal (12)   160
Blake Hutchinson (12)   161
Oliwer Maka (12)   162
Molly Marsh-Groogan (12)   163
Niamh Reid (13)   164
Naoise McDonnell (12)   165
Zeke Hopkins (12)   166
Alanna Dewar (12)   167
Thomas Irvine (13)   168
Duncan McMullan (13)   169
Declan Higgins   170
Ben Erdis   171
Leanne Magill (12)   172
Oran McClintock (12)   173
Emily McAllister   174
Erin McGinley (12)   175
Emily McNaughton (12)   176
Damien James McKillop (12)   177
Ellie Hunter (13)   178
Neil McLaughlin (13)   179
Ellie McDonnell (13)   180
Oisin Toal (12)   181

St Mary's Christian Brothers' Grammar School, Belfast

Niall Gary Morrell (14)   182

St Mary's College, Londonderry

Alyssa Campbell (12)	183

St Mary's Grammar School, Magherafelt

Tomas Doyle	184
Aodhan James Heaney (12)	185
Caroline O'Kane	186
Anna Hurl (12)	187
Patrick Kevin Glackin (12)	188
Nicholas Cleary (12)	189
Conn McAllister (12)	190
Michael Mooney (12)	191
Caitlin Craig (11)	192
Dearbhla Quinn (12)	193
Ultan Tomas Mallon (12)	194

Torlands Academy, St Thomas

Cameron Newport Snell (14)	195

THE MINI SAGAS

West Virginian Hills

The BOS squad had left the Prudwin to go on a field trip to the West Virginian Hills. The scorched had re-emerged from their hiding spot in The Mire and were infecting the locals. Once BOS arrived, they jumped from the Vertibird and started shooting rapidly.

"Mira, come in."

"I'm here, Danse."

"Have you seen Colonel?"

"The rookie?"

"No... I think he's in the Verti-"

"Yup, I'm shooting the minigun!" Colonel interrupted.

Suddenly a super mutant beneath crashed through the horde of scorched. "My God... Colonel, Danse, fall back!" Mira screeched as she was crushed. They both said, *"Run!"*

Ben Davison (12)

Belmont Community School, Belmont

Hawaii Horror

Blood had splattered over the beach. The creature was already contaminating the sunny, tropic paradise of Hawaii. Everyone was enjoying their holiday but now their brains had exploded like a bomb over the innocent pineapples. The citizens tried to escape - it was their mission but sadly, barely anyone survived. The creature was pounding through their skin, devouring their veins, crumbling their bones. Why did it have to end like this? It was awful! Demolishing watermelons, coconuts, bananas. Nobody could cope. Everyone dead and nothing left. Silent city. Steady sea. What would happen next in the horror paradise of Hawaii?

Eve Ward (13)
Belmont Community School, Belmont

The Apocalypse

As the sky turned from blue to black, deafening screams came from only metres away. Two friends hid underground in their secret bunker they built as children. If you're confused about what's happening then this is what happened...

Two weeks ago a chemical reaction happened in an old school. Ever since then, zombies have been roaming the streets. There was only one way to escape. Leave the country. Zombies surrounded the bunker. All of a sudden, a loud screech was heard. One month later, they arrived in Spain. The disease hadn't spread there. Unfortunately, most humans had traumatically, gruesomely died.

Lucy Byles (11)
Belmont Community School, Belmont

Death Penalty

Catastrophically, cars crashed, crushing people against buildings - erupting violently with flames as they did. The sound of ambulances distorted as sounds of shrieks and cries drowned them out. Suddenly, I was abruptly struck forwards onto the pavement. That's all I remember...

I woke up, drips attached to my arms. Slowly, I started to recognise the blank walls of Durham Hospital. Why was I here? Running out of the hospital, I was charged with death. Devastatingly, all I saw were the faces of people I knew... only they weren't the people I knew. They were something else entirely, non-human actually.

Mae Stephenson

Belmont Community School, Belmont

Hidden Mysteries!

A mistake by the Nazis once forgotten. Hidden at the bottom of the Mariana Trench. Isolated from the world until now. The world's infected except one country: Wakanda. Wakanda is centuries ahead of the rest of the world. Isolated from the world by a technological cloak.

The only way to detect the infection is to see if their right thumb isn't human. No cure exists. One option remains. Stop these superhumans from being created. This virus spreads through normal contact. Their right thumb is the source to their shapeshifting powers. There's one way to kill them; chop their head off.

Thomas Temperley (12)
Belmont Community School, Belmont

The City That Is Dropping Like A Fly In Fire

The human race is getting devoured. The people are slowly turning into a zombie apocalypse. It's making the unthinkable happen. Around 63 million people have turned into a zombie. This is just the beginning... This massacre happened on 31st March 2111. People are disintegrating, food is going down fast. No more water, no Wi-Fi to ring people, *no more homes!* Will London ever overcome this or will we all fall? People can't go to a different country because the virus has already covered three-quarters of the world and is not slowing down. Will we ever survive the massive outbreak...?

Harvey Starkie

Belmont Community School, Belmont

Terror Baby

Sweat trickled as Eva kicked inside my tummy. Terror! She was coming. Pushing, I used every muscle... Eva was born. Holding her close with my trembling hands, her head lolled. I stopped dead. I heard someone's footsteps in the dim light, a pale white face loomed before me; swollen, sunken, red eyes. Bony hands tore Eva away. Tears trickled rapidly. A desperate longing for Eva. His bared teeth sunk into Eva's flesh; she let out a strangled cry, before transforming. My legs failed and I collapsed. Someone was behind me. Someone was breathing. Someone had bony fingers on my shoulder...

Jessica Sophie Stewart

Belmont Community School, Belmont

Nuclear Chickens Take Over

The last survivors finally emerged from the dusty underground bunker, a horrific sight met their eyes. Nuclear chickens had taken over. A year ago, the nuclear chickens came from deep outer space seeking revenge on humans. There was no cure, just complete hell. The chickens were covered in green, luminous feathers and evil, crimson-red eyes which could shoot lasers. They contaminated people through scratching and pecking. They were destroying everything; there was no hope. Everyone was exhausted because it had been a year of starvation and thirst. This might be the end of the human race...

Jack Bradford (12)

Belmont Community School, Belmont

Gas

The gas is spreading across the city fast. Most of the population are infected - it's deadly. All of the remaining survivors are stuck in the abandoned factory. The infected don't know we're in here. They are green and have a red scar across their body (weak spots) which we have to shoot to protect ourselves. If they touch us it's over. Many of my friends have been infected but I've got to carry on to survive. Everyone wears a vest with dead nuclear substances attached. Oh no, they've found us! It's dangerous but everyone needs to fight. They're coming...

Molly Pinkerton (12)
Belmont Community School, Belmont

The Fallen

Choking, gasping, suffocating. Everything was contaminated and nobody was safe. Deadly chemicals at every corner. Breathing wasn't a privilege we had. Gas masks were our only option. However, it wasn't permanent. Gas masks meant no eating or drinking, so it was only a matter of time before we all died from starvation or dehydration. So, now all we have to do is wait and spend time with loved ones whilst we still can. It's traumatising, we're forced to watch, as peoples' eyes roll back and they fall to their death. I don't know much, except our fate is to die...

Charlotte Jorja Whitney (13)
Belmont Community School, Belmont

Project Man Eater

Apple has brought a new phone out that can connect to anything, like TV, Xbox and anything else in the world, but it's too cheap - £95 cheap! No one knew that a special bomb carrier was carrying a nuke that was not safe. It was transported away but something shot it down and the nuke was activated... It came shooting down straight in the Apple's power station... It was all absorbed up into the power lines... The green electricity zapped into the lines. Green energy went all over Durham's country. Ways to spot them is to... *Growl!*
"Aaargh!"

Benjamin Vickers (13)
Belmont Community School, Belmont

Hopeless

The giant, poisonous cloud rose into the sky, the first that week. The very first had come thirteen years ago and had triggered the apocalypse - bringing with it the infection. The infection had killed over half the population and the few that survived hid in bunkers, deep underground. Praying to a god that didn't exist. The grey-eyed creatures could be heard moaning from deep underground. Despite how long it had been since the first plane dropped a barrel-bomb filled with toxins onto the city, a cure still hadn't arrived. We were slowly dying, I feared that I was next...

Jorja Cooper (12)
Belmont Community School, Belmont

The Cure

The rash was spreading, pulsing, hurting, the cure had been ongoing for over fifteen years. Windows were covered and no daylight was allowed through, not even a chink in the curtain. It was like an asylum. Hell on earth began to unfold, whoever was caught in the daylight was eliminated. Without realising; a chink of daylight gapped through the curtain, causing me to feel something scuttle under my skin. The contaminating disease had spread even more, all I could hear was screams. If I'm gone and whoever is reading this, you should leave, it's not safe here. You will die.

Tegan Mia Cockbain (12)
Belmont Community School, Belmont

Are You There?

"Ouija, are you there?" We'd come back to the place we started. *Smash!* Looking to the left, the cross had fallen. It'd gotten worse. We were the last survivors of this apocalypse. The first time we were here, we'd set the spirits free. They massacred everyone, minus us who started it. Why? We were going to find out. "Why keep us?" we asked. The planchette moved, spelling out 'so we can end it where you started it'. Blood dripped down the wall, drawers flew open, knives surrounded us. We heard a low growl.
'Kill'...

Molly Doolan
Belmont Community School, Belmont

A Shopping Disaster

The world has descended into chaos. A deadly virus has spread through the food and water supply that turns people into brain-dead zombies. There are not many people left, bodies are piling up. One group of people are barricaded in a supermarket. However, they have been there for days and the edible food has run out and they're getting desperate. Some have tried to leave but failed. Their final way of escape is a food truck behind the supermarket, they've considered their options and it's the only way. So they run out the door, get in the truck and drive...

Daniel Hubar

Belmont Community School, Belmont

World's End

On the twenty-seventh March 2019, it all ended as Earth was engulfed in toxic rays from what used to be humanity moving around, doing their daily business and having fun with all of their friends. But now it's a desolate place, full of lifeless zombies. It turns out the government had poisoned the water supply and turned everyone into lifeless zombies. The best people on the planet were in a bunker underground. They tried to get out and fly away but the amount of zombies overwhelmed them, they didn't last long. Now the whole world lives under zombie control.

Ash Kilford (12)
Belmont Community School, Belmont

Blood Trouble

Scientists were searching for the cure for a deadly disease. The test subjects had the disease but were on the brink of death. Each subject got their cells mutated in a different way.

"Test Subject A is unaccounted for," spluttered a worried, young trainee. When they found him, he seemed to act odd - so did the whole village. The strange man had cuts and scabs all over his body. Stupidly, the scientist took a sample of Subject A's blood, without any equipment. As soon as that blood touched his hand, he froze and his eyes bulged and turned red...

Ellie Jennings
Belmont Community School, Belmont

The Cure Is Here... Somewhere

The cure had to be here somewhere... Matt hurried in a panic, pulling numerous bottles from the drawers. My arms gradually giving way! The poisonous rash was spreading, pulsing, hurting as I held up the door, determined to not let any of those hideous, repulsive creatures get in. Suddenly, the door slammed open. My eyes blinded; the sun emerged. I looked at the ruined city, decaying bodies obscured the ground. The menacing growls echoing in my head while I saw what was before me. But I was already dying. I hoped Matt could find the antidote and get himself out.

Katie Robinson
Belmont Community School, Belmont

The Dire

The government alongside scientists have put together an experiment to create a treatment for dementia with the hope that it goes well... However, they used a dog to test it on, it had no effects. They had begun giving it to humans... An old man turned into a mutated werewolf. Whenever he was near something, the mutation being described as the 'dire' was spread to them. Eventually, after around a month or two, the dire had been spread out to almost whole of the United Kingdom's population and wasn't stopping there, the dire was spreading fast!

Harrison Sutherland

Belmont Community School, Belmont

The Deadly Infection

A world infection spreads. No one knows how it came but it's a bad infection because it kills. The infection spreads and kills about 1000 people because of this infection. A scientist tried to discover a new element but it became a deadly, dangerous infection. The deadly infection has been here for a week and 2725 people have been contaminated. Who knows how many days we have left. Scientists are trying to make a cure but I think there isn't enough time. Could this be the end of the world? Or could scientists find a cure for this deadly contamination?

Leo Dineen
Belmont Community School, Belmont

Rise Of The Mutant Monsters

The man woke up in the cold, empty room. The only light was coming through a singular closed window. The only things in the room were a chest of drawers and the cryogenic freezer. As the man looked outside, he saw blood splattered all around the outside of the bunker. As he opened the drawers, he found a note that said 'Apocalypse, find food' in scribbly handwriting. New clothes were underneath the note. As he put them on, a piercing scream filled the air. As he went outside, a mutant monster greeted him. Before he could blink, the creature attacked!

John Lyons (12)
Belmont Community School, Belmont

Zombie Apocalypse

The zombies were slowly spreading all over the countries. Nobody could get access to the cure for the zombie bite. Once someone got bitten, they could turn anyone into a zombie. The only way to avoid the disease was to keep everyone away from each other. Families locked themselves in houses and blocked off all the windows and gaps. The zombies couldn't get into the houses. But before they knew it, they needed to get food. Some people went to get some to keep them all going. As they took their first step into the shop, they weren't seen again...

Roma Lee (13)
Belmont Community School, Belmont

Untitled

Test Subject A, who was unaccounted for, tipped over petrol cans. This could cause serious damage if it were to be set on fire. Many people had been reported dead or missing. Roughly one million people were around this area during this tragic event. Approximately half of this huge number had been reported dead. We needed a way to stop this from happening as soon as possible. Many people were going to be left homeless, jobless. I was losing signal, I didn't know what to say. The world ended, there was nobody left and the zombies took over the world.

Kaydee Rose Wilkinson (13)
Belmont Community School, Belmont

Red War

The warhead struck the coast; it caused a tsunami that devoured most of the western seaboard, causing numerous earthquakes and deaths in the millions. Then they started getting sick. Red bulging sores all over the body, thick mucus-filled blood coming out of the nose and mouth. It was horrific. People just fell on the street and started convulsing on the floor with blood coming out of their ears. The best doctors and scientists were losing sleep trying to study it. Nothing could be done. It came from that warhead. It was everywhere. There was no cure.

Samuel Treweeke
Belmont Community School, Belmont

The Apocalypse

The human race was slowly and suddenly becoming extinct. If you got scratched or bitten you became a zombie. A lab experiment had gone wrong! It was happening now, you would only have a little time left. Suddenly, a chemical reaction blew up and invaded every person, turning them into a zombie; you still had a chance as people were running to safe houses underground. It was currently happening in Durham city centre. The giant poisonous cloud rose into the sky and people became infected. I reached into my pocket to find a weapon! My advice is run, now!

Rhianna Margaret Ord (13)

Belmont Community School, Belmont

O2 Oxygen

Scientists have discovered a new toxin that has mysteriously appeared and is wiping out the whole state. The only safe place has been confirmed and it is above the clouds, oxygen levels are running low and people are getting contaminated by these awful toxins. You may find you're the only one up there, most others have fled the country in need of non-toxic air. We are trying to clear the air and make it a liveable place again! Stay safe, take care of yourself. Scientists will get back to you once the air is clean. Be careful, it's spreading.

Macy Gray

Belmont Community School, Belmont

Zombies Destroy The Human Race

In recent days, 95% of the human race have been infected from the chemical-filled air. To make matters worse, any scratches or bites will infect you. The government has luckily set up a dome around Durham to protect the remaining survivors. Unfortunately, ammo is running out, food is running low and the dome is weakening. If they break out to restore the human race, they will be infected from a bite or infected gas. If they stay, they will either starve or be infected from the damaged dome. Either way, it seems like the human race will be destroyed.

Callum Blakey

Belmont Community School, Belmont

The Infected Survivor

Boom! The infected spread through the streets. I was shipping high tier weapons, I grabbed a gun and was ready. On the radio, the government said, "We are going to drop a nuke to kill the zombies so all survivors get to the bomb shelter in Tilted Towers!"

I started sprinting but a zombie dived on me. I pulled the trigger and it fell to the floor. Its blood splashed on my face...

I made it to the bunker, the nuke dropped. Everything had a red tint.

Suddenly, I was desperate for blood. I was infected. "No!"

Ethan McLaughlin
Belmont Community School, Belmont

Zombies

Ally and Sam were visiting their dad, who's a scientist. He was telling them how his illness, that he created, had been put into effect. Holding the container filled with flies covered in this deadly illness, he chucked it out the window. He let out a mad cry and turned into a hideous zombie with shrivelled skin. At the terrifying sight of this monster, the two kids screamed. The kids ran at the door - more zombies! It looked like the whole city was turning into monsters. Ally and Sam were surrounded. They didn't know what to do except cry.

Isabella Blackburn (12)

Belmont Community School, Belmont

The Disease

The human race is slowly disintegrating as a life-threatening disease has broken loose, everyone in the world has been evacuated to protect us as it is our only chance. Many people have already died as there is no cure to survive. Shops have been looted and crops aren't growing - the world is falling apart. The longer we try to survive, the more we will suffer. Yesterday, another lethal bomb exploded and a pile of corpses surrounded it. We didn't realise that a small earthquake could cause a life-threatening disaster. Will we find a cure?

Molly Rose Donaldson (12)

Belmont Community School, Belmont

Descending Death

After a long prison sentence (for murder), I finally escaped. The electric had cut out so all cells opened, the other inmates were acting strange; they were growling and were now pursuing me. I ran. I ran so fast that I collided with the wall of darkness.

When I awoke, I felt something crawling under my skin! It felt like hell. I was home. I suddenly lost control, my skin rotted, bugs scuttled away, I was a zombie. My mouth opened and my zombified body reached my healthy family. There is no worse pain than murdering and eating your family.

Kyza Ralph (12)
Belmont Community School, Belmont

Renegade Raider

The disease RR has hit London and other capital cities. Already, three billion people have been infected, only one hundred million have died to this massacre. Every survivor is going to die out due to food resources going low and we can't feed everyone all the time. We have no communication at all to talk to the outside world. With this dome above us, we will start to find it hard to breathe and die of suffocation. The number of deaths increases every minute of the day. Will we survive this terrible massacre or will we perish like them...?

Oliver Mitchell

Belmont Community School, Belmont

Zombie Attack

After the nuclear explosion, everything was destroyed. Suddenly, a mysterious fog appeared from nowhere. A really drunk man walked into the fog and got infected. He saw another person and gave him the disease. The only way you could tell they were infected was by the eyes. They would change to a grey colour. One person looked carefully at the infected person and saw that he was a zombie and realised there was a zombie apocalypse. By the time she looked again at the zombie, it was chasing after her. She ran and ran but came to a dead-end...

Rhiann Ward

Belmont Community School, Belmont

Horrendous Gas Attack!

We finally emerged from the underground bunker. The air felt thick with the poisonous gas. I wondered who'd burst the gas pipe. They must feel bad for nearly wiping out the whole human race! The smell was horrendous and extremely pungent from the dead animals and corpses. I was starving as I had not eaten in four days. There was barely any food as all the plants and the supermarket food was contaminated as well as the water from the taps. This was not good. This was terrible. This was horrendous. What was going to happen to all of us?

Abigail Carr
Belmont Community School, Belmont

The Resistance

On March 17th 2050, a nuclear outbreak has scarred the planet. Anyone caught in the radiation is dead. They become flesh-eaters, I hate their beaming blue eyes. I'm part of the Resistance, we defend our safe house in New York and clear out rooms day in day out. We've been fighting the infection for months but I don't know how long we'll last. I have seen many friends pass after the attacks and they're picking us off day by day, one by one. If I'm honest, I think we're dead in a week and there's no chance...

Matthew Scott

Belmont Community School, Belmont

Untitled

We finally emerge from the underground bunker after two months of darkness and claustrophobia. My son and daughter have to sleep on blankets and pillows. We have been down here to stay away from a giant mosquito. Everyone the mosquito stares at in the eye will immediately fall to the ground. The giant creature has nearly wiped out the whole of Durham. If we step outside, we will most likely die but if we stay in here, we will eventually run out of food and we will probably die of hunger or dehydration. I just hope my kids will survive...

Jamie Greaves (12)
Belmont Community School, Belmont

Infected

Something scuttled under my skin. It gave me a rash and I began to panic. I immediately ran to the phone for help. No answer. I screamed and began to shake. Looking out the window made me shocked. There were undead swarming my neighbourhood. "It's a dream, it's not real." I scurried to my basement, proceeding to pick up planks. I quickly barricaded the doors and windows. A second later, I saw something under my skin again. It was some kind of worm. I felt it climb to my brain. I screeched as I became one with the dead.

Lucas Short
Belmont Community School, Belmont

Nuclear Nightmare

The human race has contracted a rare virus that no one had ever dreamed could happen. It all started when a scientist had started to create a cell using the particles of a nuclear bomb. After the explosion, we rose from the underground bunker; we saw the dead rising. They were covered in black and green scars from the nuclear explosion. The air stung and the ground was hot. The creatures were crawling around and groaning. No one would survive! Just then, my arms grew black and green scars. It was up to the fittest to survive...

Ella Reay-Carroll
Belmont Community School, Belmont

The Disease

The human race has come to an end. It is a contracted disease which has spread all over Britain. The government has covered Durham in a colossal dome to protect us, but then someone out of nowhere became a zombie and bit me. I could see the purple, poisonous germ spreading through my veins. Next thing I knew, I became a zombie. Then they tried to cure me but there was no luck, then a doctor found something on the floor and they tested me. The last drop fell into the test tube. My blood was orange; contaminated and poisonous...

Jacob Hamilton
Belmont Community School, Belmont

Parasites

Something scuttled under his skin. His eyes turned black and his skin turned pale. Parasites moved around his body. He was helpless. I ran away from him. My legs couldn't move fast enough. I felt him chasing me. My heart was beating fast and I began to hyperventilate. He caught me, grabbed me and bit me. I felt the parasites form under my skin. I felt my eyes turn black and my skin turn pale. I felt parasites move around my body. I was helpless. I saw her. I ran after her. I bit her. Parasites formed. She was helpless.

Millie Lisgo
Belmont Community School, Belmont

Poisonous Powder

Children screaming, mothers crying, family members grieving as babies and toddlers are coming out in huge red boils. They have found poisonous powder in baby formula. It all started 3rd July 2060, when a mother gave her child a bottle of milk before her nap and the child woke with red boils all over her body. The mother quickly rushed to A&E where they said it was a rash that would go in 4-6 days, but then a news report broke out saying that there was poison in baby formula. Baby milk has been off shelves for days...

Eve Berriman
Belmont Community School, Belmont

How Long Will It Last?

We finally emerged from the bunker, everything was silent, no noise in the whole town. One year ago, everything was normal, everything was happy, everything was calm. I was starving, I hadn't eaten in several days and needed food quickly. The first thing that came to my mind was had anyone else survived? This disease had spread by the water supply to the town, this had turned everyone into flesh-eating zombies and destroyed most of the human race. I think I'm one of the last humans left. How long will this last?

Alfie James Howard (12)
Belmont Community School, Belmont

The Wreckage

"Ughh!" My head was ringing like a phone. As I peered over the wreckage of the crash; my eyes were met with an apocalyptic and barren wasteland. As I emerged from the wreckage, I was ambushed by a horde of 'walkers'. I was pinned to the ground as their jaws latched onto my flesh, I let out a blood-curdling scream. I passed out. When I awoke, my body suddenly reanimated. I lost all control, except my mind - where I am documenting this. I now walk amongst the 'dead' or so we all thought...

Joel Maddison (13)
Belmont Community School, Belmont

Terrible Terror

More than 90% of the human race has been wiped out due to a very contagious disease. Only a few groups of people have survived. There's only a limited supply of food left. We think the cause of this zombie apocalypse is a toxic chemical spill. The only way to get contaminated is if you are bitten or scratched by one of the zombies. Lots of people are trying to get away but it is not possible because there are too many zombies coming from every direction. No one will survive the terrible zombie apocalypse.

Luke Dante Mason
Belmont Community School, Belmont

DNA Slipped!

All was going fine when I was trying to find the DNA for a man who had paid £100, I was mixing the chemicals together to try and get the right substance. Then, I must have got the wrong liquid and before I knew it, the whole lab had exploded! The chemical started to get on peoples' skin; it was so irritating. I could feel it burning on my hands and arms. I already knew it would never go away. The rash was spreading, pulsing, hurting... We needed to separate the people. This was it! We all knew it!

Ella-Rose Searle
Belmont Community School, Belmont

My Sons Heard My Scream!

We finally emerged from the underground bunker. There had not been life around anywhere. There was only me and my sons. My father, wife, brother gone. The forest looked dark and empty. My sons looked up at me and I knew what was there. Hell was surrounding us, hoarding around us in a big pack. I spotted a gap in the horde. A scream sounded behind me. I whacked the zombie with my bat. I pushed my sons through the gap and told them to run. I lay down and thought as hell closed in. My sons heard my scream!

Jenson Carter (12)

Belmont Community School, Belmont

End Table

I woke up in my cosy studio apartment to a knock on my door, I looked at the clock, 8am, I was going to be late for work. I shuffled to the door, opened it with a creak and revealed a worn-looking table. I had never ordered a table and had no idea how it got there.

Closing the door behind me an hour later, I left for work, the table was gone...

On the way, I heard a scream... inside a tree? Upon arriving, my boss told me that a deadly parasite had infected inanimate objects to come alive...

Kayla Slee (12)
Belmont Community School, Belmont

The Metal Dome

This virus was made by a mad scientist. He was doing some tests on a mosquito. It went terribly wrong and the scientist caught it so there was no cure. Durham was the only place that wasn't infected, so the government put a metal dome over Durham. Since it was metal, there was no light. We all have been in this dome for two years. All we were given was a list of symptoms like: skin won't heal, lose control and many more. We are running out of food. We all will die unless we can find a cure...

Katie Walton
Belmont Community School, Belmont

Nazi Zombies

In 1946, the war had ended and all that remained was the dead. Me and other people had emerged from the bunker 2 or 3 weeks later. Around the bunker were rotten corpses. We decided to stay there for the next couple of days then set out to get materials and search for a new home. The reason why they were here was because the Germans tried to use them to win, but it didn't work out for them. When we set off, we encountered a horde of zombies, until we had no choice but to try and sneak through...

Charlie Napper

Belmont Community School, Belmont

People Turn Rogue

We finally emerged from the underground bunker. Suddenly, the sky turned black and people were rising from the dead. We realised that the research that the lab was doing must have contaminated real humans. To save the human race, we must get to the lab and find the cure or else the whole world would end. I remembered one of the scientists saying it was in lab 3421 and there would be a bottle that you had to inject into one of the undead people and the human race would not be infected anymore...

Harry John Cooper (13)
Belmont Community School, Belmont

Shadow Of The Earth

Trees drooping as I ran from the shadow. It had been taunting the world. This was not a single person, it was an alien organisation trying to get rid of the human race. I was trapped, they took everything from me. As I was running, I came to a field so I tried to hide from it. As a huge lightning bolt ignited the sky, there was more looking for me. I managed to find a bunker and survive for a few days, suddenly the electricity went out. Food was a limiting factor, I had run out. I was doomed...

Evan Bland

Belmont Community School, Belmont

Zombie Invasion!

A zombie attack has just happened in Durham, the factory where people worked has just exploded and the gas is spreading everywhere in Durham. The army is trying to evacuate everyone from the city before they get infected too. I got out of the truck and the army started to shoot at the hill, they told me to run because the zombies broke out of the dome. Now, the full country is going to be taken over by the zombies. Then suddenly, the zombies are surrounding me...

Caine Michael Blakeley (13)

Belmont Community School, Belmont

The Fallen Ones

"Did you hear the news?"

"No, why? What happened?" I then turned on the television, I saw horrific live footage... the news presenter explained what happened.

"There was a breach at a facility in Swindon and a highly contagious virus was released. Those infected have symptoms of enlarged, black eyes and the victims mutilate their own faces, carving smiles on them. Those contaminated make weird gurgles and screams. They are called The Fallen Ones."

All of a sudden, there was a bang and I jumped through the window, but they were outside, we were too late...

Jack Martin (15)
Carrickfergus Academy, Carrickfergus

Our Rotten World

Our world is rotten. Literally. People like myself are trapped in our somewhat 'clean' city. Meanwhile, the unfortunate are roaming around rotting as we speak, on the outskirts of our city. Where the 'clean' live it's raised up by about twenty metres with a huge wire and glass dome protecting us from the disease-filled air that lurks outside. The disease is named 'Mors Putredine', Latin for 'death by rotting'. 100 years ago, the animals we ate gained an infection from what scientists say was caused by global warming. To our dismay, this is our life now, forever.

Kaitlyn Beggs (12)
Carrickfergus Academy, Carrickfergus

My Time To Hunt

Something scuttles beneath my skin... blood and foam fill my lungs, restricting my breathing. The sound of my pulse fills my ears. *Pump-pump-pump;* growing louder and louder, until it's all I can hear. My eyes glaze over, colour draining from my vision, leaving only blues and greens behind. The scuttling stops. Maggots burst out from my face, tearing the skin as they wriggle down my neck. Murderous thoughts flood my brain; the images of tearing skin beneath my teeth, blood filling my mouth. I feel adrenaline run through my veins. I am ready. It's my time to hunt.

Hannah Walker (16)
Carrickfergus Academy, Carrickfergus

Solution

Bloodthirsty, infected, banging, demanding the sweating scientist's flesh. As he tried to save himself, he rushed the test tubes to the infected blood samples. Rushing, he dropped them. Time slowed down as he was in terror, as the solution for the cure smashed, like a water balloon hitting the ground. The thick, syrup-like substance scattered on the floor. The infected desperately tried to break through the reinforced glass, craving his flesh. The glass started to give way as the scientist cowered in the corner. They got in. The scientist was dead, the cure was no more.

Jude Meehan (15)
Carrickfergus Academy, Carrickfergus

Red Ice

In Canada, 2039, we have androids. They look human and sound human. It's revolutionary in technological advancements. The downside was the chemical in androids made a deadly drug called 'Red Ice'. It was a drug that you burn, it trips you out, but what happens if an android took it? It starts a war! It messes the software, it's like mad cow disease, they attack everyone: humans and androids. Detroit is the only place that doesn't have androids. Canada is now gone to android deviants. Other countries are gone. Is this the end? Have androids really won?

Carrie Caitlyn Clarke (13)
Carrickfergus Academy, Carrickfergus

The Deadly Cloud

The giant, poisonous cloud rose into the sky. Take a breath outside, you're dead, take a step out in the rain, you're dead. This is deathly! One single droplet of rain will make you deadly to everyone. This vicious, violent virus is taking thousands of lives and is making innocent people criminals by spreading it from person to person. Nobody is safe. Lock your doors, don't open your windows and protect your family. Beware of others. The dark, gloomy cloud is so determined to swallow you up and spread the virus. Help your fearful self before it is too late!

Joanna Finlay (16)
Carrickfergus Academy, Carrickfergus

Undiagnosed

We had her strapped down, but that didn't stop the infection spreading. A large mushroom cloud formed in the distance; the war still continued even though we would all die. We turned back to horror, she had turned greyish black and her veins seemed as if they were tying her up, tight, bulging and dark, she screamed in pain... or was it hunger? Her eyes turned black and her mouth stretched to double its size. Her nose bled a black liquid. "She's gone!" said our leader as he raised a loaded gun to her head. "Rest in peace girl..."

Rabeka McMurtry (16)
Carrickfergus Academy, Carrickfergus

They Have Arrived

"Mission Control. This is Agent 7-6-4 requesting back-up, they are here-"
"Hello? Hello? Agent 7-6-4? Are you still there?"
That was the last thing he ever said... No one knows why they came, how they got here or what they look like. Everyone they encounter they kill on sight. They are a complete mystery. How do we defeat an enemy when they are completely invisible? Humanity is at stake here and no one knows how to save us... "Someone send help, we are defenceless against them. Someone teach us how to kill them..."

Jessica Allison Cully (13)

Carrickfergus Academy, Carrickfergus

Closed Border

It has been months now since the disease started, and different countries have had different ideas on how to keep the disease out. Northern Ireland's choice was closing the border and having tight border control. They are rounding up the sick and shooting them, they say it's the only way. No one is allowed in or out, at the border you get shot on sight, and because of this we only rely on the food we grow here, but that's running out rapidly. I don't think anyone will survive the disaster because of this tight border security. Many die.

Ewan Beattie (13)

Carrickfergus Academy, Carrickfergus

Poor Nurse Brannigan

It started with a parasite. A parasite which Doctor Vandelstein never intended to make; a parasite which led to the end of humanity as we knew it. It leapt from the test tube and onto the first life source it could find, which happened to be Nurse Brannigan. She began itching, scratching, clawing at her skin and screaming for any source of relief which would make the skin-crawling creature stop. Fortunately for Nurse Brannigan, the parasite was done with her, however, that was only when her face turned blue and her lifeless corpse hit the floor.

Rachel McFarland (15)

Carrickfergus Academy, Carrickfergus

Mission Contamination

A nuclear blast goes off in Canada, creating what is described as hell on Earth. A massive nuclear fallout cloud blacks out the sun, turning people into zombies by infecting them with nuclear fallout. The zombies walk together into the night, infecting more people but, when they get to the Burns family, the Burns run and jump into their secret underground bunker. When they get in, they see that some of their food and water has been stolen. They realise that they are going to die because their food and water supplies are rapidly depleting.

Ben Picken (15)
Carrickfergus Academy, Carrickfergus

Blue Hands

A doctor walked out of his study, pale-faced. He had been trying to save a man's life for hours. However, it was in vain. He stepped forwards carefully. Bodies lay on the floor. People thought that there was some sort of virus. He agreed. He thought this because the sick were turning blue... The doctor ran out panicked, sweat poured from his face. He had quite a temperature. He took a cigarette out of his pocket, lit it and started to smoke. He looked at his hands. His cigarette fell out of his mouth. They were turning bright blue!

Aiden Cameron (13)
Carrickfergus Academy, Carrickfergus

Killer Air

The giant poisonous cloud rose into the sky. What no one knew was that it was filled with liquid acid. Every time it rained, the acid would fade away into the air and would then infect the air. Children would run in the streets, thinking they were getting fresh air when really the air was destroying their insides. Mums and dads were already infected as this contamination had been going on for decades. The reason no one died straight away is that the acid took seventy-eighty years to actually shut down our organs and body parts.

Ashlyn Boyle (13)
Carrickfergus Academy, Carrickfergus

Feeding Ground

A new host. A young woman. I leave the elderly body into the younger, healthier one. Ohhh. Her skin is so succulent, so sweet. Couldn't ask for a better snack. I begin leaving my mark on her. This one will last longer than the last. I won't have to move on too soon. I begin to feed. I'll savour this one. I send my mark out, cover more ground, become more powerful. This one could have gone far in her puny world, but my family needed more meals! Imagine, creating a race just to starve them! We'll wipe them out.

Aimee Patricia Walker (16)
Carrickfergus Academy, Carrickfergus

The Others

We called them the Others. They arrived here on Earth four years ago and have settled here ever since. Four long years filled with constant fear. They started hunting us humans down shortly after they arrived. One by one. Slowly disposing of us all, until the Others were the only ones left. You never see them during the day; they prefer to hunt us in the darkness and the deafening silence that the night provides. No one knows exactly what they look like. No one has come out alive after an encounter with one of the Others...

Jodie Shaw (16)
Carrickfergus Academy, Carrickfergus

The Rash

The rash was spreading, pulsing, hurting everyone that got it. It was very contagious and a lot of people were getting infected. It felt like a pressure on his chest when the rash started to thrive and he was starting to lose his vision. The rash was itching and burning and spreading all over his body. The man saw the same thing happen to someone else but quicker. He started panicking because of what was happening to people. The rash was hurting everyone. As the rash spread over the world, there were only a few survivors.

Ben Rees

Carrickfergus Academy, Carrickfergus

Madness

They thought locking me away would contain my madness. They were trying to break me but little did they know, I snapped a long time ago; that's why I'm here in this room with four padded walls. You call me crazy, I call myself unique. I didn't kill anyone but all the evidence pointed to my hands that had a strange red tint and the brown substance on the bottom of my shoe that you could only get from being in the woods. They thought locking me away would contain my madness, but I can feel it spreading.

Dylan Franklin (16)
Carrickfergus Academy, Carrickfergus

Tiny Spider But Deadly Spider

Hi, my name is Jonas. I am currently in hiding because the country has been overrun with a disease that is killing everyone. It all started from a tiny little spider, the size of your fingernail, that was brought over from a foreign country in a fruit. Ever since that day, there has been a drastic increase in deaths and the population of the country has already gone down about a quarter of a million! I have been in hiding for about three weeks now and I'm running low on rations. Will I make it out alive?

Jonas Benjamin Barnley (12)

Carrickfergus Academy, Carrickfergus

Zombie Apocalypse

A deadly zombie virus has been unleashed by Dr Contamination. The virus is spreading to the population at rapid speed. My family and I haven't got the virus yet and are running out of options. There's a safe zone a mile away with enough supplies to last all of us one year! The only problem is it is close to the centre of the town which is more dangerous. We need to leave now! We set off on the journey and later come across a ton of zombies who chase us to the safe zone, but we all get there...

Callum James Close (13)
Carrickfergus Academy, Carrickfergus

Rain Contamination

It was during school, my dad came running in, he pulled me out and put me into the car. I'd never seen him drive so fast. He drove us into the woods and up to an underground bunker. On the side was a computer for his handprint. Inside were all the rooms in a house and enough food for us for years. Later, Father left us there, Mother went to find him. One drop of rain hit her and she fell to the ground. Dead.
We were in there for years. Food was running low and we had no time...

Carla Brown (12)
Carrickfergus Academy, Carrickfergus

Test Subject A

"Test Subject A is unaccounted for. If you have any information, please conta..." The voice stopped, crackled. Doctor Bernard realised the broadcasting room was two rooms away. He panicked, frozen with fear, confused and vulnerable. He was thinking of getting weapons but he would get spotted. Bernard knew what Subject A was, but couldn't describe its strength. He decided to head to the basement, being as quiet as possible. He heard a loud bang, frozen with fear, *Bang!* Again, Bernard didn't move a finger. The bangs got louder! They stopped... It darted towards him, *slash*, dead! Bernard, finally, relieved.

Kyle Jackson
Coleraine Grammar School, Coleraine

Last Of Our Kind

I woke up on the cold concrete ground. Nobody had houses anymore unless you could afford them. Most people I knew couldn't. Only the rich were 'safe', but corruption had long since overtaken their minds. Nobody was safe. It was either death to the parasite that had wiped out most of the population or losing yourself, reaching the near brink of madness. Neither were curable. The unnamed parasite had no cure and meds never worked for those who broke. You'd be lucky to be well and healthy. I was lucky. I, Keri Trisha Black, was in danger... grave danger...

Clara Macy McNicholl (12)
Coleraine Grammar School, Coleraine

The Cloud Rises

The giant poisonous cloud rose into the sky. The city went into complete chaos. Cars crashed, people ran and buildings collapsed. The experiment to stop global warming had failed. It came closer. I had to run. I ran, ran and ran but had to come to a halt as the Atlantic Ocean stopped me from going any further. The clouds came closer and I saw hundreds of people getting caught by the clouds and dropping dead. There was nowhere to run. I panicked but came to the conclusion that it was over. The clouds arrived, I accepted. My heart stopped.

Thomas Brown (13)
Coleraine Grammar School, Coleraine

Terror In The City

The giant, poisonous cloud rose into the sky above the great city. The whole city was trapped in its purple, infectious death trap. Could this be the end of the human race? Surely not? The cloud seemed to grow bigger, towering over the citizens as they watched on in fear. It seemed inevitable that this was the end. Scientists ran out of ideas. They didn't know how to stop this giant, purple beast. As the panic started to spread like a rash, suddenly there was a bright flash of light, the cloud had vanished. The citizens rejoiced!

Jack Embleton (13)
Coleraine Grammar School, Coleraine

The Insidious Infection Of The Insanely Ill

The rash was spreading, pulsing, hurting... my arm bled as I scanned the room, searching for a first aid kit. *Thump... thump... thump...* the bangs of an infected on the window, attempting to get in. Was it going to get in? Thundering gunshots echoed throughout the building. I held my gun shaking uncontrollably as the rash stung a million times worse than before. My heart skipped a beat every second as gunshots echoed! The test subjects had escaped! Humanity was doomed. I tightly wrapped the bandage around my arm, pouring disinfectant substances over the rash, then it got worse...

Madison Ogle (15)
Craigavon Senior High School, Lurgan

Butterfly Skin

I stood my ground behind the glass window as their weakened bodies slammed against it like a pack of desperate mutts. Grimacing as their peeling flesh left a trail against the window, I turned and faced my new home. A room full of different appliances, chemicals, and other... necessities. With a sigh, I caressed the crying girl's cheek. She was healthy, she wasn't even phased by the creation. I wanted to know why. I tried all different manners to find out why of all creatures she was immune. It was time to dig deeper. I slowly grabbed my precious scalpel...

Weronika Mroz (15)

Craigavon Senior High School, Lurgan

Safely Insane

Caged, we have been imprisoned for years. Trapped within walls, these stupid, god-forsaken bricks. They are supposed to keep us safe from the monsters outside but what about the ones in our heads day by day? I go a little bit more insane! These demons have ruined our lives! Our homes destroyed, our families tortured and killed before our eyes, our friends murdered in cold blood. These will keep us safe, but what's the point of being protected, living without any freedom? This is why I'm leaving... leaving this world, there is no hope for us anymore... no hope.

Cara Calvin (14)
Crumlin Integrated College, Crumlin

The Clown Effect

In 2001, Chicago was gassed and now is left to rot away. Just days before that, everything was normal, people were going to schools and work. On Friday 21st January, all hell broke loose. Everyone was enjoying the amusement park, there was a Ferris wheel, a frisbee ride etc. Jonathan, Nicole and Jemma all had low self-esteem so they decided to get clown masks and gas everyone so they felt just as ugly as they did. I was on the Ferris wheel, they were gassing everyone. Now Chicago is abandoned. Just memories left. Our faces are deformed.

Taylir Costello (12)
Crumlin Integrated College, Crumlin

The Safe Room

His rash was spreading, pulsing, hurting. He was in so much pain. He wouldn't say but his face said everything. The chunk the zombie took out of his arm had caused a lot of blood loss and he was fading fast, there was nothing I could do about it. This made me really sad and annoyed, so annoyed I started throwing things around the safe room. Then I realised, if I mixed up some potions maybe, just maybe, I could save him. I mixed, shook and heated potions but nothing worked. The world was crumbling down around me, doomed!

Lucy Elliott (12)
Crumlin Integrated College, Crumlin

The Plague

I was running as fast as I could, the wind blowing my long, blonde hair. The zombies were catching up, I ran into an abandoned shop. I boarded up the windows and door but the smoke was coming! The zombies tried to break down the door. I climbed out through a crack in the wall, I was running down the street, suddenly zombies popped up and attacked me. I took my knife and stabbed one in the head. It fell to the ground, its head bleeding, arms disappearing. I started to run again, I had found a place to stay!

Ella Falloon (11)
Crumlin Integrated College, Crumlin

Infection's Wrath

"It's time. Ready the missiles."
"Yes, sir."
Harry marched towards the launch station
hesitantly. Through the reinforced doors of the
Infection Prevention and Control Centre (IPCC) he
could hear Major Max crying. No one wanted what
was about to happen, but humanity depended on
it. For years, they had used the Isles of Scilly as a
quarantine for an extremely infectious disease. But
then a member of staff got infected and... Harry
shuddered. He couldn't bear to think about the
bodies lying on the floor. As the growling got
louder and louder, he started coughing. He was
infected...

Kenny Gibson (12)
Five Islands Academy, St Marys

The Infection

It had begun. The rash was spreading, pulsing, hurting. I was hiding behind barrels of blood, hoping not to be found. My heart was racing like a race car. I was scared! My leg was cut, and my body was cold all over. Could that mean I was infected? What if I was? If I was, I would be roaming the streets. So I couldn't be. Something grabbed my arm. It was a zombie that started the infection. My arm was cut. The last drop of my blood dripped out... I was now part of the infection.

Emily Hobbs (11)
Five Islands Academy, St Marys

The School Plague

Today, everyone was ill. A haunting bug ran around the whole school. There were only three people, including me, in the whole school. This was nasty, like the plague. There were doctors with masks that made them look like birds. Was this the plague? Fortunately, I was not infected.
The school was so quiet. There was only one teacher now (a maths teacher) but I thought she was getting it too. There must be a cure somewhere. I looked around, it was empty. It was just me!

Ava Elizabeth Joan Kearsley (11)
Five Islands Academy, St Marys

Corruption

I had been running for hours on end, but I knew if I stopped they could catch my scent and I would be done for. I had to reach the bridge before them. I could only just see the first wooden pole when I heard the unmistakable crunch of the virus taking over a child cell by cell. I had to go or I would never have the chance of saving my family. I reached the bridge and leapt onto the wood only to hear a great crack and the wood gave way beneath my feet. I fell, screaming.

Hafwen Bryher Kendrick (11)

Five Islands Academy, St Marys

Death Virus

We were in the lab, trying to find a cure when something went wrong. My boss fell and dropped some chemicals in the tube. Smoke started to rise. The alarm went off and the power shut down. It was pitch black. There were flashing green lights and I heard awful screams. I touched a wall blindly and a door opened and locked me in a secret room. I pulled my phone out of my pocket to contact my family but, before I could do that, a message popped up saying, 'Death virus in Northern Ireland - Stay indoors!'

James Church
Groomsport Intensive Support Unit, Groomsport

The Unforgivable

The beaten, depressed, hopeless soldiers trudged through the camp, guided by the malevolent, glorified Nazi soldiers. The darkness spread through the camp like a disease. The lab stood like a rose in no-man's-land, hiding the terror and pain that lay within. Dr Van Ginkel raised his voice harshly. "You, my sinners shall witness what happens when DNA is tampered with." His crazed eyes were filled with flames.

A disgusting creature was dragged in front of them. They cut the beast's chains and it charged forward.

"Time to die!" the Doctor cried angrily.

Darkness overwhelmed them. Their time was over...

Henry Wayne Gibbons (13)
Haileybury Turnford School, Cheshunt

The Water

"The spillage can't be real, right? The water doesn't even taste unusual."
Little did she know she was slowly losing vision.
Every person from work and her family thought she was crazy.
"You might not ever see again, you keep drinking that vile, contaminated tap water!"
But no one knew she was correct. Half the population went blind, all because of the polluted water. When she woke up, she couldn't even tell the colour of her own hair.
"Argh! What is happening?"
She searched through her room on her hands and knees to find her phone and call her mum...

Mackenzie Warren (12)
Haileybury Turnford School, Cheshunt

Extinction

Her slow nod was the conclusion of it all. "Release the gas. There's way too many of them."
The London Eye and Big Ben began spewing poisonous, green gas. Everyone ran, fearfully, but there was no hope. One after the other, people tumbled on top of each other. The population numbers went from ten million to a couple of hundred within minutes. The deadly gas spread like uncontrollable wildfire.
"There's no running from it, citizens of London. You're all dead!" the Queen's voice boomed over the extinct city. And she was right, we were all dead, all except one...

Lelde Voita (12)

Haileybury Turnford School, Cheshunt

Red Sparrows

Confusion. Confusion is the only expression on my face as I look around the misty roads.
Alone.
That's my second feeling, as the normally busy streets are as quiet as a mouse. Making the short way to my street, the soft wind tickles my face, feeling soft and light, reminding me of a feather. Realising that nearly all houses around me are in complete destruction, I go to the closest house with a light shining.
I should've been more careful. Getting dragged inside, there were labs where people are trapped and being injected, others scratching at the glossy glass. Appalling.

Kirsty Dewberry (15)
Haileybury Turnford School, Cheshunt

The Connection

"We can't kill her," I said angrily.
"If she dies, they all do."
Tony looked at me, eyes wide. I sighed, heavily, tears in my eyes.
"Six months ago, the rest of the injections got contaminated by her. I never said anything because I wanted it to be true. Her DNA is in them. The others can be contained but she cannot. She dies, this all goes down. They're connected."
Tony rubbed his eyes.
"What about the storage unit?" he choked. I looked at him, tears streaming down my face.
"Tony... what are we going to do?"

Mackenzie Paulding (12)
Haileybury Turnford School, Cheshunt

The Perfect Boy

The power plant was the focal point of California. Everyone knows the name, everyone knows why. Jen's perfect boy. Long fawn hair, clear skin, and big blue eyes, yet no one felt attracted. She made her own solution. Business was booming.
Then Clifford snuck in at 1:02 on the Monday morning. He located the simulator and sniffed out the chemical, potassium. Threw it. Ran. Ducked. *Crack!* The simulator broke. The next morning, she woke up and drove to work. But, as she opened the door, a test tube laid there dripping on the floor. The place was contaminated.

Amy Richardson (14)
Haileybury Turnford School, Cheshunt

Twin

My twin... The body on the floor didn't give me the sense that I should be scared. Hair messy. Skin was dark grey. Holes in his face. Clothes ripped. Me and two others stepped over the crime scene tape. I went back in. The body disappeared. All was left was a note: 'Find me, 2pm S-Lab'.

Confused, but intrigued, shaking and heart pounding, I went into the room. He bit me. A zombie! I knew I was turning. He told me something in his croaky voice. He told me words I'd never forget.

"You're my twin!"

Amazed, shocked. My twin...

Courtney Cioffi (15)
Haileybury Turnford School, Cheshunt

Perfume Gone Bad

He sprayed perfume onto the girl as she turned around. Her eyes went wide and she screamed, "I love you!"

She started hugging the boy and it was his dream come true. He looked up, seeing the perfume fly into an air vent.

"Oh no!" he said as everyone in the room started chasing after him.

About four hours later, he was sitting on a roof watching everyone turn into praying mantis, trying to rip his head off. He whispered to himself, "What am I going to do?"

Suddenly, a giant praying mantis climbed up, straight for him.

Toby Sharples (13)
Haileybury Turnford School, Cheshunt

Danger!

"I have almost finished my creation!" shouted the scientist.
"I can't wait to test it!" he said to himself, laughing. The scientist picked up his potion and walked towards the little lizard that was in the cage. He poured the potion onto the small, helpless lizard. The small, green lizard grew. It burst out of the cage and made a horrible noise, as loud as a plane. It hit the defenceless, old, idiotic scientist and he flew. The lizard had not only become large, it had become smart, agile and quick. The lizard had run away. For now...

Lewis Butteriss

Haileybury Turnford School, Cheshunt

Nuclear Outbreak

Nuclear outbreak sparks the end of humanity! The air's clean, for now. The water is fresh, for now. It's all on me. Australians, gone! Siberians, gone! Europeans, gone! It seems like the end of the world but it's not too late! All I need to do is make enough gas masks for the whole of America. The entire nation is in great trepidation. The shops have sold out. The bars are empty. The houses are full. It's coming. Everyone can sense it. The strong aroma of nervousness fills my nostrils. We're on our own. For now, it's all or nothing.

Billy Fairclough (12)

Haileybury Turnford School, Cheshunt

The Classroom Invasion!

Turnford High School had been invaded with deadly, brain-eating monsters. Classroom 8AC, which looked spotless, was in use. Mid-lesson, the people had started to act differently which meant that the infection had spread. The plague had been overtaken. This was now the worst infection which would spread everywhere. Class was over and the zombies came out from their hiding places to kill the whole school. Students' screams could be heard and the entire city could hear it. Looking out of the window, the school was ruined and could never be the same again!

Aimee Jordan (13)
Haileybury Turnford School, Cheshunt

Revenge

By the time it got to the sixth child feeling unwell, Mr Smith quickly realised that there must be something seriously wrong. Children were being violently sick all over the dinner hall. Mr Smith quickly realised all the children eating the same food were the ones being sick. He immediately took charge of the situation by stopping the cooks from serving any more of the affected food. He needed to find what was causing this situation. But how? The food was sent away for testing, where it was discovered someone had poisoned it. Was it a cook or a child?

Ruby Lincoln (11)
Haileybury Turnford School, Cheshunt

The End

I took a step forward, peering at the jars of specimens. As I placed my hand around one, out of nowhere I heard a voice from behind me. I quickly rotated round and knocked the jar off the shelf.
"Is anyone there?" I fearfully called.
I took a look at the shattered glass on the floor and saw the specimen was missing... I took a step back.
"Run!" I heard someone whisper from behind.
I started to walk back before I sprinted. But I was too late. Smoke started to fill the room. Before I knew it, I blacked out...

Tom Garcia (12)
Haileybury Turnford School, Cheshunt

The Outbreak

One day in the lab, there were two scientists. They attempted to create and modify a virus that could be used to fight wars so that lives would not be lost. They had been working on this virus for many years but never had a breakthrough. Then, something went wrong. They injected a mouse with the virus. It had died, they thought. While disposing of the dead mouse, the virus had contaminated everything, turning everyone in range into a mindless beast. Now we are the last humans remaining, fighting for humanity. This is humanity's last stand...

Flavius Ionut Ghita (15)

Haileybury Turnford School, Cheshunt

Infected

Four days. That's how long I have been hiding. This disgusting, infected scratch that will end my life. Who would guess that the main scientist of an organisation to stop this would be stupid enough to get scratched? Lost. That's all I can feel. I'm slowly losing my mind and I don't know what to do. I can feel my heart get slower as it sinks in. *Thump, thump.* Over and over. I'm as lost as a child who'd let go of its mum's hand. My eyes slowly close as my sanity is ripped away from me. Then, I'm gone.

Kitty Elizabeth Piper (13)
Haileybury Turnford School, Cheshunt

The Horde

I had been trekking for days now. The infected had been following me the whole time but it's here, the core of the infection. Ever since that fateful day, when I lost everything, my only goal was to destroy the horde. One arrow, one shot, one chance. All I could hear was their broken screams and agonising screeches. The base was deep underground. Every hall was swamped by infected who were ready to kill. The core, pulsing and glowing, the centre of it all. I had been trekking for days just for this chance. I aimed, I fired, I hoped...

Isaac Shallow (14)
Haileybury Turnford School, Cheshunt

The Infected

The rash was spreading, it was everywhere, except here. We were safe. For now... We were locked in by metal bars creating a gate of the strongest metals we could find. It felt like a prison and we hated it but, it was either this or death. The infected would always stand pushing against the bars, trying to grab us through the gaps. A small girl walked towards the bars when no one was watching and the infected grabbed her and dragged her through the bars. They bit her and she slowly transformed. She died, but lived on through memories.

Ellie Newman (13)

Haileybury Turnford School, Cheshunt

End Of Time

A meteor is heading to Earth. The meteor is breaking and spreading a deadly gas around the world. The rivers are poisonous. When it rains, all that falls is acid. If it touches you, you're dead. Dave was driving back from work to get shelter as it was about to rain. He took an alternative route to get there quicker. He received a text from his wife. Without looking at the road, he crashed! His car went flying off the road. *Splash!* He'd landed in the river. The toxic water filled the car. This was it. It was all over.

Alexander Alderson (12)

Haileybury Turnford School, Cheshunt

The Zombies

There were zombies every corner I turned. I saw a cottage so I went in. *Bang!* A zombie crashed into the wall. I took a step closer then there was a grunt. When I took a step back, there was another grunt. A black figure turned around with chemicals all over it. I asked him, "Can you help me kill the zombies?"

Bang! There was a crack in the wall. The figure was making a potion. The zombies were making the crack in the wall bigger. The figure was nearly done but suddenly, they were in...

Lily Clayton (11)
Haileybury Turnford School, Cheshunt

The Rain

It was a normal day at school, not knowing anything about the future. I was practising for my exams in my English class. In the next five minutes, my dad appeared and said, "Come fast!"
I came out of the school and got in the car with my sister. There was a huge black cloud. I kept asking, "What's happening?" Dad just said to keep calm. We got to a forest where there was a bunker. The rain was a virus. As it poured down, my dad fell down. I screamed and saw my sister die in front of me.

Bruno Hascec (13)
Haileybury Turnford School, Cheshunt

Substance

It was dark and the streets were quiet. All the street lights were off... I was on my way to a corner shop on the edge of a street and I heard a scream. It came from the abandoned hospital. I ran to see what had happened. I burst into the hospital and the lights were flickering and a purple substance was on the floor, it was kind of sticky substance. It came from the testing room. I tried to look for the people that screamed but something found me first. It was the purple substance...

Heyden Sookaree (13)
Haileybury Turnford School, Cheshunt

Injection 1.0.1

On the 11th day on the 4th month, the government introduced a new injection for children. They lined up one by one to get the injection that was needed. Remember, this was only for children. They all got it and a few days later, everyone was getting infected, adults and teens of all ages died because of this virus in their homes. A few managed to get away from the mess and survived another day without getting contaminated. What will happen next?

Pelayia Panayides (13)

Haileybury Turnford School, Cheshunt

Hordes

Security breach detected, shooting, screaming, bleeding. Squadron and teams have failed to contain death and pain. You'll go in fear. Creatures and entities are starting to kill, no wonder why! The moronic and the acute, the small and the tall stand no chance. They lock the doors and lock the gates in a futile attempt here. They keep coming but fall soulless into the red licking ground. They break out, they come in hordes, waves, and pain. People are seen to be set on fire. Hopes and dreams are unreachable here.

Jose Noah Sollano Monghit (13)

Hazelwood College, Newtownabbey

The Horrendous Rash

The rash is spreading, pulsing, hurting. The pain is climbing up my leg, eating away at my flesh. It feels as if my leg is going to fall off. It's as soft as a pillow with blood flowing through it. I have been clutched by massive, ferocious hands and I am seeing black stars. I am now in a ship filled with monsters. It is like an army battlefield. The walls are filled with blood. I have been badly beaten and they are now amputating my disgusting leg. I am gasping for air. What's the world come to?

Caoimhghin McAtamney (12)

Hazelwood College, Newtownabbey

The Plague, You Can't Escape It

Symptoms of emptiness, regret, helplessness. Students replacing eye contact with self-depictional humour, the jokes a welcomed normality. Smiles drop one by one. Everyone's infected by the merciless silent killer. Conversations are a formality, automatically dismissive. Cutting, smoking, sniffing. We can't escape it. How do we free ourselves from the shackles of this epidemic?

Words hang at the tip of my tongue, brain half empty like the veins of hell.

I sit beneath the willow tree, among the fallen leaves. This is where I'm meant to be because no one else wants me. I can't escape it.

Sara Ipakchi (16)

Hockerill Anglo-European College, Bishop's Stortford

Calling All Teens

"A viral disease is spreading like wildfire! Adults dropping dead by the second, it seems that any children under thirteen aren't affected but..." The news announces on the radio, then I hear the reporters fall to the ground with a sickening splat. I stare at the director in fear, I know she's next. Everything feels so slow as she thuds to the ground and the orphanage erupts in fits of screaming and sobbing. "We must leave right now to figure out how to stop this disease. Find a cure... wait." I pause, trembling. I'm fourteen, why am I still here?

Sophie Crawford (14)

Loreto College, Coleraine

Virus

Viral, he thought. *It's going viral*. This was it. The start of a new world, where he was in control. Soon, Cobra would be on every device on the planet, every phone, laptop and tablet connected to the Wi-Fi. With the touch of a button, he could make all technology on Earth do his bidding. He would have everyone's passwords, images, videos and message logs at his fingertips and everyone on the planet would know him as the most powerful man in the world. Nobody would ever dare to hurt his little sister. She would finally, finally be happy. Forever.

Grace McConnell (14)

Loreto College, Coleraine

Buggies

The container left a strange noise in my already creeped out mind. I was in a death bug cure research room, trying to finish a cure to bring back my friend, Sam. He was bitten last Tuesday by what scrappers call... Buggies, strange, zombie-like creatures that have been infected by the death bug virus. I searched units, checked computers. I was there for almost two hours and found nothing that could save the world from mass extinction. Then I heard something from the distance. "Ugh!" There was a blood-curdling scream. There it was, a buggy slowly creeping over to me!

Leo Carmichael (12)

Penrice Academy, St Austell

WWIII

Sounds of firearms echoed through the ashes, engulfing everything we knew. Nothing mattered but survival; through the chaos, the smell of death arose. Adrenaline pulsed through our veins as we charged towards the safety of our sanctuary. It was too late. Sound was erased from the face of this godforsaken world as the mushroom cloud appeared. My first instinct was to call out, "Jordan!"

There was no sound...

Then, out of the toxic breath of Hell, emerged Jordan. I thought it was my first hallucination from the radiation. His skin had vanished and his limbs blasted off.

"Why God?"

Jack Chimes (14)
St Christopher School, Letchworth Garden City

Cities

Death stalked the streets with its scythe. Nobody was spared. Dead bodies piled up in the road, rotted in the mid-summer sun. The stench wafted through the alleys, infecting anyone who smelt it. Disease was rife in the world. Everything died. Everyone died. Yet we kept on dancing, dancing like the Devil himself. Death was our only spectator, clapping his bony hands when somebody died. His skull clattered with laughter at our misfortune. Laughing at us. Laughing at our souls. I lept elegantly, pivoted and fell on my knees. I fell onto my stomach before death. Nobody could escape Strasbourg.

Poppy Holden-Adams (14)

St Christopher School, Letchworth Garden City

Bird's-Eye View

Everyone is frail; the plague is slowly eating our planet away. Now the street is sealed off, no food arrives and the water is sparse. Carts pass by the windows stacked up with bodies. The world is full of young, bright people with futures now unrecognisable. Depression is at its peak. It is devastating to see children being born into this catastrophe because there is no hope anymore. A tear smudges the lens of my telescope. Although I am alone, I step back onto the red rock and realise how lucky I am to be up here on Mars.

Archie Holt (13)
St Christopher School, Letchworth Garden City

Donkig

I find myself in the middle of the road, just standing there, doing absolutely nothing. I'm unable to move and unable to yell, I can just see. I'd rather die than see it. I stare directly at a cross between a pig and a donkey. I'm not sure whether it'll kill me and whether it will be slow. I think I'll probably find out soon enough. I'm right. I find myself being eaten up into the wet mouth of a donkig (donkey and a pig) as I soon find out who the monster really was: me...

William McGinley (11)

St Christopher School, Letchworth Garden City

The Gas

In 2020, a gas was released. It seeped through the street and washed over everything in its path. No one knew where or who it came from, what people did know was that it killed. After four days, the gas had gone and taken nearly everything with it. The small speckles of land quickly crammed with survivors and too became useless. People got desperate and, when people were threatened to lose their life, they left all.

Johnny Haase (14)
St Christopher School, Letchworth Garden City

Operation Chimera

Truth or consequences. The Chimera virus spread like wildfire. The Spetsna and GIGN managed to contain the virus, and deployed the RGCBRN unit to extract Dr Martyn. The incessant ghouls of the husk-like creatures grew louder as we travelled through the streets devoured by an inferno and the live spike-like piles protruding from the body. Red, burning skin. Extremely aggressive behaviour. These symptoms had been explained during the briefing. This was no ordinary virus, it was a parasite-like creature which manifests inside a host, causing strange mutations. Anything could go wrong with only one wrong, contaminated breath.

Louis Manchip (13)

St George Catholic College, Swaythling

Breathless

The infection's approaching. It ruins the minds of innocent humans. An infection that leaves you with shivers, yet you wouldn't know how you felt because with this infection you're not you. You will be controlled by the Master. The girl was breathless in her own sweat. They were coming. They grasped her neck, pulled her to the ground and suffocated her until she had no pulse. The touch of their hands changed her life. She wasn't Zoey Catler from Brighton anymore. She was like everyone else. Her life didn't actually matter. She was just an anonymous creature, searching again...

Olivia Redmond (12)
St George Catholic College, Swaythling

Planet Toxic

Planet Earth as we know it is slowly dying, releasing harmful gasses into our air. Breathing is now a challenge. Anyone who unfortunately breathes this chemical will immediately fall, cold. With everyone dying, the government has collapsed. Population has fallen and all the scientists have rocketed off to Mars. Livestock is all dead. No food is left anywhere. People slump around the pathways, blaming our generation for this tragedy. Nevertheless, we never give up. We will never surrender! No matter how long it takes to fight this, we as a race will live on and will never surrender to anyone!

Katie Hunter (11)
St George Catholic College, Swaythling

Contaminating The World

The rash was spreading, pulsing, hurting and overtaking my weak, helpless body. As darkness overtook the castle, I screamed, although it was silenced by the ominous clouds hovering over the ancient castle. My family were trapped there. The contamination enveloped the castle and everyone was isolated in there. Well, except me, no one knew about my uncommon disease, but I didn't want to be locked up from the world. The cloud started hurling lightning at the castle and thunder boomed deafeningly. I rushed into the castle, not remembering the world behind me. I contaminated the entire world.

Toni Euler-Ajayi
St George Catholic College, Swaythling

Radioactive Potion

"It's okay boy, it's me..." Growl...

It all started when Doctor Lazaraus created a radioactive potion. It was very complex. From the corner of his eye, he could see a mysterious figure lurking in the shadows. Suspicion filled his veins. Who was it? Was it a spy or a secret agent? He asked, "Who are you?"

However, there was no reply! The enigmatic silhouette dashed to the potion. A million questions were in Doctor Lazaraus' head. He wasn't sure what to do but he knew that it was too dangerous for anyone. Abruptly, the test tube broke and split...

Joash Siby (12)
St George Catholic College, Swaythling

The Apocalypse Hierarchy

It happened suddenly, in 2001, a strange comet crashed into the surface of the Earth, causing an impact so strong, cracks appeared on the Earth. This made the weather go haywire and heavy rain fell every day. This made the water levels rise so that most continents were submerged with catastrophic results. But a bigger problem came to be. This environment gave geese the perfect living conditions and thus, they realised that they were now superior. Millions of people died and the geese became humanity's biggest enemy. I fear that this is the end and now I must say... farewell.

Dawid Kwiecien (13)

St George Catholic College, Swaythling

Contamination!

The human race was long forgotten. Death, after death. Disease, after disease. The humans died out. Arising from their coffins, creatures emerged. Boneless. The blood rushed up my veins. It kicked in. They were zombies! I was trapped in the moment of time. Scuttling up my spine, a tingle of disgustingness flooded over me, causing me to panic. It sunk into my skin, causing infection. Blood, sweat, tears. The yellow muck engulfed me. Disease was spreading to every human. I killed the planet. I was a murderer. The last drop of poison fell into the test tube. It was complete.

Isobel Linda Louise Moran (12)

St George Catholic College, Swaythling

The Cloud

It happened that day. The gaseous cloud of impending doom webbed from one country to another. Running, panting, I hoped the spider didn't catch me. The thought of death wrapped itself around my head; squeezing out any form of happiness. Then I saw it. The yellow face chomping its way through anything in its path. It surrounded me. I held my breath and counted. Ten, nine, eight, seven, six, five, four... I paused. Thinking of my family and friends but nothing could save me now. I exhaled. Then inhaled. A powerful surge of toxins spread throughout my body. Then death.

Ruben Luca Blaise Aburrow (12)
St George Catholic College, Swaythling

The Apocalypse

The year is 2059. MI6 has just discovered what was causing the death of billions. Top scientists announced for all human beings to barricade themselves from the outside world. PX26 have already killed the world's most powerful people. Team leaders have fallen and I am the last man standing. The apocalypse has just begun and soon, I will be infected and all is lost. It's an eternity in Hell! We are being erased! The Devil has won the battle.
Suddenly, a blinding light killed my sight. It was deafening. Darkness was all around me. Now we have nothing at all!

Evan Jay Sayas (12)
St George Catholic College, Swaythling

The Claws Of Death

We're dying. No help. No hope. The human race is sure to die. The only escape from this hell is death. Every second, thousands die in this cloud of poison. The only survivors are living underground. Eventually, we'll die, crack up and show ourselves to death. No food to grow, the cloud destroyed our crops. I've tried to go out to die but my friends won't let me, they're still fighting strong. Every day checking the door for mist, we haven't had a problem yet, but today, the cloud was seeping through the cracks, almost melting the stone. Goodbye!

Reuben McDermott (12)

St George Catholic College, Swaythling

Virus Z

The world twisted and turned around me. My senses failed, leaving my vision blurry and my ears ringing. I made out some movement around me and I could only make out fragments of words, such as, "Test Subject... insecure... contamination." I groaned in pain, realising something was growing inside me, and it was trying to claw its way out. Vomit spilt out my mouth, the taste making me cringe. Figures circled around me, injecting me with needles and trying to stop whatever it was that was feeding off my insides. I screamed as the creature clawed its way out...

Maksymilian Slonka (13)
St George Catholic College, Swaythling

Wrath

There wasn't any use in trying to save us: we were doomed. The bunkers offered some protection, but they always found ways in, pulsing, wriggling, squirming. They were like maggots in cheese, boring through the warm flesh to dispatch their offspring, but they found no use in the dead. Corpses were stacked up outside and still more were being put down for experiencing the yellowing skin and bubbling flesh. We thought we'd survive when we were put in the only wrath-proof bunker. It was cold. We were hungry, but we were safe. That was before my skin went yellow.

Bronwyn Springett (12)
St George Catholic College, Swaythling

The Death

The shadow was colossal. The death cloud suffocated the air, poison dropped into the apocalyptic world. Acidity burnt the jungle as a knived creature stared with its red eyes straight at me. Its pocket was loaded with four magnum revolvers. As if in slow motion, his gun flicked out and shot me right in the nose. A stream of dark red blood covered the disgusting, damp ground outside of the overgrown city. I was knocked unconscious a second after.

When I woke up, my flesh was green. Wait, it wasn't flesh, it was blood. I had changed into a zombie.

Pablo Tombaccini-Maestro (12)
St George Catholic College, Swaythling

The Attack

It's finally the summer holidays. There was a camping trip with all of my school friends at school. Everyone was lining up to show their tickets. As soon as I got on the bus with my friends, I was already talking about how much fun we were going to have. After we arrived, we organised everything we went and had smores and marshmallows. We were telling stories until we heard a scream in the woods. Something ran towards us. Something sharp bit me and everyone was attacked by zombies. My skin was turning green, then my vision started going blurry...

Gabby Markelyte (11)
St George Catholic College, Swaythling

The Hole

There we were, hidden under a carpet in a hole. People were dropping like flies after one small insect carrying malaria had infected everyone. This hole was our only chance of surviving; if we stepped out, we would be dead. The carpet was our shield, protecting us from the disease. Even we were vulnerable, anything small could crawl into the hole and we would have been nothing but a few more corpses of the countless deaths. Was this our only hope? Were we going to survive? We sat there, thinking if we were going to get out of this alive...

Raphael Garcia (12)
St George Catholic College, Swaythling

Winchester

Heart racing, lungs aching, I ran through the streets. The streets which were once filled with vibrant shops that cascaded the houses with sweet smells. That was all the past. Now they were just rubble, bombed by the merciless Nazis. As I ran through the thick, polluted air of Winchester, I started to slow down as I encountered a boy. He seemed much younger than me and seemed to be lost but as I neared him, he vanished. Vanished? Then once again, I saw but as I neared him he vanished. This time he didn't vanish. Instead, he turned...

Nevin Biju Joseph (13)
St George Catholic College, Swaythling

My Day Of Dread

I lay there flat, prostrate, hurt. It was throbbing. Adrenaline was helping, well - sort of. The pain was bad, but knowing that I could die from this deadly bite worried me even more. My mother told me I looked pale. She was worried, I was worried. I told her to take me to hospital, she said, "No, let's wait a few minutes and see if the pain goes away." I didn't argue - I wasn't in the mindset to be talking constantly for no valid reason. The pain started once more. It was bad, really bad... Then, I fainted...

Oscar Sadler-Abert (12)

St George Catholic College, Swaythling

The Curse

The curse crept ever closer. I sprinted down the long, narrow passageway, the zombified humans hot on my tail. I'd been camping alone when they came, holding pitchforks and flaming torches. If they touched you, you became one of them. As far as I knew, I was the only human left. I had been with someone else, they couldn't keep up. That was the last I ever saw of them. They were coming, getting ever closer. I was within their reach. They came out of nowhere. I couldn't move, then I realised they had already grabbed my arm...

Joe Oliver Stockley (12)
St George Catholic College, Swaythling

Contamination

Contamination. The world was at its worst. Every living thing was half dead. Every single street was full of bacteria and disease that could make you go mad. It started off April 1982, most people were full of rashes. They kept growing every hour from the poison in their bloodstream. Less than two weeks later, everyone was hallucinating. After a month or so, their brains started rotting away and all that was left of them was a decaying carcass. In less than a month, I was the only living human left in the world. The end of the world.

Leo Thompson (11)

St George Catholic College, Swaythling

Trapped

There is a disease. It's killing everyone. The only humans left are stuck on a remote island off the coast of Australia, trying to find a cure to stop this nightmare. However, it is looking like there is no end in sight. Yet, there are infected bodies trying to reach our hideout, to see if there is a cure that simply doesn't exist. No one can escape from reality. Nothing can save us. Our food is finishing, the water is salty. We are barely surviving. We have nowhere else to go. Everywhere is infected. Everyone will die...

Zaina Anwar (11)
St George Catholic College, Swaythling

The Hand Of Doom

It was a normal, dark Friday night.

"Come on Isobel!" Isobel was only twelve but she seemed to enjoy stealing. She was accompanied by a boy. His name was James. This time, they were taking it too far. They were robbing a shut down chemical factory. As soon as they got in, James' hand got a taste of an unknown substance capable of world domination. It took over him and all good things were gone due to one punch to the ground. So now I welcome you to a new world, a world of dark, evil corruption, rage and doom.

Caleb Fairman (12)

St George Catholic College, Swaythling

The Cloud

The giant, toxic cloud came to England and killed a lot of living things like animals and humans. The cloud could kill everyone and everything in less than a minute. The gas could burn everyone to death, slowly and painfully. Then everyone rose as vicious, bloodthirsty zombies. If you were in an underground bunker, there was no point in hiding because it would find a way to enter your bunker. The side effects of this toxic cloud were that it would burn you to death and make you vomit. The only way to escape was to leave home.

Claudio Araujo (12)

St George Catholic College, Swaythling

Storm

A giant cloud had blocked the sun for some time now and I was starting to get worried. It's almost like we were trapped in a bubble, just trying to get out. As I looked up into the darkness, I saw rain thrashing down. But this wasn't just any rain, it felt like acid. The rain covered me from head to toe. It started burning my skin. I screamed. I saw dark shadows coming towards me. A thousand thoughts filled my head. What was it? What were they doing? They were getting closer. I started running. There was no escape...

Chloe Longfellow (11)

St George Catholic College, Swaythling

The Boy In The Dome

There he stood, frothing at the mouth. Suddenly, everything was so much darker than it was when it arrived... The atmosphere was so much more, lethal feeling... I was grateful that it wasn't my family who was infected by this disease. I watched the boy in the glass dome. He looked scared. I wanted to let him out... I felt sorry for him. I didn't want him to suffer in there alone. My eyes shifted to the large, crimson button located on the side of the dome. My hand was drawn to it. I pushed it. The disease was out...

Grace Lily Robins (12)
St George Catholic College, Swaythling

The Zombie Infection

It's spreading around my city as I'm trying to stay away from the outsiders on my road as cautiously as possible. Later in the evening, I look out my window. I see, quite clearly, green goo on the roads and on cars and trees. Then... I see a person getting attacked by zombies. But then when I look carefully at who this person is, I find out that it is one of my relatives... That night, I cry myself to sleep and when I get up in the morning, I call for my parents and they don't respond. They're infected...

Bethany Quester (12)
St George Catholic College, Swaythling

Apocalypse

Screaming spreads through my once quiet town. As the zombie apocalypse kills hundreds a minute, worry spreads on the faces of the remaining few. I bravely leave my house to go feed my donkeys and I realise I am too late because they already have the dreaded infection. Mr Jones, my favourite donkey, bites me. I have to rush to the medicine cabinet to disinfect my leg, but my leg is too bad. I'll have to chop it off. I flip out as zombies attack me, so I grab the nearest weapon. I die, so there are no more civilians.

Toby Lucas
St George Catholic College, Swaythling

Death

I wiped the cold sweat off my forehead. The disease was spreading and killing, stealing our family. We were not safe anywhere. If I went outside, I was dead. If I stayed inside, I was dead. If I moved, I was dead. I hunched nearby the window, not daring to look outside, at the state of our world. My blood rushed through me like a river. Lives were dissolving every second. Everything suddenly became distant and blurry. No, I can't pass out. I was the only person left alive in our world. This disease means death.

Lydia McLoughlin-Parker (11)
St George Catholic College, Swaythling

The Cure

The last drop fell into the test tube. All hope was gone. They had the cure. I ran off into the woods in anger. I climbed up a tree and wept. Insanity shouldn't have the cure. I needed to somehow go back in time and change the outcome. Suddenly, a gold light appeared on a branch. It gave me a weird feeling. I felt like I needed to touch it. I got closer and closer and then, *whoosh!* I was back, watching them grab the cure. I ran into the test lab and snatched the cure out of their hands.

Matthew Hamblyn (12)

St George Catholic College, Swaythling

The Zombies

Mutant creatures surrounded us as we crawled back into the bunker. Eerie sounds came from above: it was the zombies. My friend had been infected so I was alone. Flesh was all I could see. I have been isolated for around twenty days, but I was still waiting for people to rescue me. I lifted the door and it was clear. So I escaped. As soon as I was out, I could hear helicopters from far away. Minutes later, I saw that they were coming for me. They lifted me up and we went to the nearest rescue base.

Danial Khan (12)
St George Catholic College, Swaythling

Deadly Poison

Poison starts, the blood stops, life goes on, but only for now. Hour by hour, minute by minute, I watched my life fade away. Everyone else was dead, all lifeless because of one man, one evil, vile man. But I stand still. I am the man and the world is mine. It shall end being mine and no one else will take it from me. Soon I will die and earth will be gone. Nothing will be in space, not even a single thing. I have succeeded. I have got revenge. Revenge is sweet, even when it takes your life.

Edward Rayner (12)
St George Catholic College, Swaythling

Acid Shot

It all started when he went to school. He walked down a gloomy alleyway because he thought it was a short cut to school. Suddenly, there was a bang. The boy ran and hid. His heart was pumping as fast as a jet. He saw a shadow around the corner then it went black.

When I woke up, there was green goo all over me. Then I realised that it was toxic acid. But the weird thing was that it did not kill me. When I got out of the alleyway, I looked around. Then it all went black.

Charles Hiscock (12)
St George Catholic College, Swaythling

The End?

A gun fires as they obtain my body. I feel blood in my mouth as they pin me down. Three months on the run has led to this. A briefcase is pulled out and I know, in moments, all emotions and senses will be lost. The bubbling green liquid is compressed into my vein. Pain - my sides open up and my teeth turn to pincers. I let out a deafening screech and my vision fades. I come to my senses - a load of scientists are monitoring me. I begin to realise this will be the end for me.

Joshua Spradbery (12)
St George Catholic College, Swaythling

Man Goes Mad

Jimmy has a rare disease, occurring when you get stressed and agitated, releasing a harmful airborne substance.

Jimmy escaped from Belfast hospital and wandered to the park where he saw a group of innocent strangers, he got anxious and viciously attacked each victim. The disease was rapidly spreading; during attacks the disease transfers through the air and passes to anyone within a mile.

Jimmy was found attacking a stray dog. A tranquilliser shot from the doctor stopped Jimmy instantly.

A medical cure and the search is still ongoing for those people Jimmy attacked, they are yet to be found...

Ann Esme McAuley (13)

St Killian's College, Carnlough

The Thing In The Dark

I was sitting in the corner of the dark room with that thing staring at me. The only sound was my Labrador breathing and a *drip... drip...* My mind was spinning with questions of why me? I haven't done anything wrong! I thought it was fake, all just some elaborate hoax! After what seemed like an eternity, the thing started limping forward, closer and closer invading on my personal space. Its face was gaunt and sickly pale. The thing spoke in a high-pitched voice. sending shivers down my spine, "Follow... without resistance and it won't hurt... much!"
I screamed.

Maggi McKillion (14)
St Killian's College, Carnlough

The Living Dead

The day was beautiful. I was strolling in the forest when unexpectedly, I saw something red flashing behind the tree, but I ignored it. Suddenly, the sky began to darken and the wind started thudding hard against the tall, terrifying trees. I decided to run back home, but inexplicably I couldn't move. Moans and groans emerged from underneath and the ground began to shake. Paralysed with fear, I started to shout. Soon after, dead bodies covered with blood rose from the underground. Suddenly... I felt someone grab my leg. Turning around, looking at the beast, I recognised my best friend!

Nikola Lawniczak (15)
St Killian's College, Carnlough

Surviving The Apocalypse

"Catherine, Eleanor, there's too many of them!"
We were boxed into a corner and our bullets were
running dangerously low.
Catherine shrieked, but I couldn't see her; there
were too many zombies. I looked over at Eleanor.
The disease was already in her blood. Her eyes
were rolling up and her skin was turning pale
green. I realised I was alone. I grabbed the
detonator from my pocket and pressed it. *Boom!*
It sent zombies everywhere. It swept me off my
feet into the wall behind me. My head was
pounding and my vision was blurry. Suddenly, I saw
her...

Tara Leopold (12)
St Killian's College, Carnlough

The Altered

After the Apocalypse War, the world crumbled. Radiation asphyxiated all life and only a meagre amount of beings survived. In a last-ditch attempt for life, human and animals began to fuse together. They became altered. Kaleb was alone when the alteration occurred. Sitting in the cove, letting waves lap over him. Suddenly, an unknown force dragged him into the ocean. Down in the dark, he struggled for air as he was presented to a mystical, luminous beast. The soul of the sea. It lunged for Kaleb, fusing itself to him. Then, their minds, bodies, hearts and souls became one...

Cara McAuley (13)
St Killian's College, Carnlough

The Hunt For Blood

Xlantasha disease is starting to spread. First, you will feel an itching, throbbing rash all over the body, a cold tingle will continuously go down your spine and your toes and fingers may start to fall off! This was made accidentally when an experiment went wrong with the spiders at the lab causing them to carry a viral disease. They broke free from their insect prison to invade someone's personal bubble. Their favourite food is blood. You will know there is something wrong when you feel something scuttling under your skin. They're on the hunt for your blood!

Ellie-Jo Butler (13)

St Killian's College, Carnlough

The Failed Experiment

"Hello class, today we are going to do an experiment. First, mix five litres of Fanta and two grams of pepper. Also, you will need some paper, about four sheets. Put these all into a conical flask and mix it. Now you try."

"Whoops, Miss, I think I put in too much paper."

Boom! The conical flask exploded and green gas spread across the classroom, sinking down from the ceiling. The students began to panic and choke. They began to change, creaking, melting and morphing into Grumpy Teachers. Only one student was untouched...

Peter McAuley (12)

St Killian's College, Carnlough

Zombie Bite

"The cure has to be here somewhere!" exclaimed Martin.

"Where could it be?" asked Rebecca.

Whilst searching the mad scientist's lab, my eyes scanned the room for the cure to zombie bites. I caught a glimpse of it and went and took it off the shelf. We went out and sprinted to my house like a leopard running for its prey. We made it. Me, Martin and Rebecca entered the house but, when we went in, there were zombies everywhere. We had to leave but, as we turned, we were circled by thousands of zombies. We had nowhere to go...

Theo McToal (12)

St Killian's College, Carnlough

How Could It Be

We were in the lab trying to create a cure to wipe out the problem. Rats have evolved from it. The glass was too strong, well that's what we thought. At roughly 1am last night, one broke out and was hiding, breeding, hunting, learning... We were scared. We kept hearing movement in the vents. Then, it attacked viciously like a lion. A co-worker was eaten. I got outside. In the vents, there were eggs ready to hatch. Right there and then, I knew this was the end. Shrieks coming from outside, people crying. Eggs hatching... attack, attack! Earth is gone...

Blake Hutchinson (12)
St Killian's College, Carnlough

Is It The End

"Watch out!" I screamed as a laser shot past my friend. Earth was terrifying now. I'll tell you what happened: a gigantic, suspicious-looking spaceship landed in New York, followed by lots of mysterious creatures. They looked like werewolves but with robotic hands and X-ray glasses. They were frightening, especially when they started shooting green lasers. If you got hit, your eyes turned black and skin dark purple. Next, they chased after people who were not yet infected. One by one everyone was changing. The human race was going to end...

Oliwer Maka (12)
St Killian's College, Carnlough

The Target

As I emerged from the underground bunker, my target was nowhere in sight. I clutched my pistol close to my chest as if it was a reassuring object, not a deadly weapon. A few steps later, I noticed a repulsive, green goo splattered across the wall.
"Achoo!" My six-year-old brother had sneezed all over me.
"Put that Nerf gun away before you poke someone's eye out!" I heard Mum shriek. My brother looked as sick as ever. I knew it was wrong comparing him to a disease-ridden-zombie, but it's all fun and games, isn't it?

Molly Marsh-Groogan (12)

St Killian's College, Carnlough

The Last Of Us

Thump. Glass breaks. "Maeve, I told you not to make noise." We run into the lab searching for a cure. Anything. "I told you this was a waste of time Ann." Then, we find something locked away in the desk. A folder. We open it, pages filled with notes. But just then, the door opens, they run in, heading straight for us, knocking over chairs. The virus made them mad. We run out of the office and down the corridor, they chase us to the end. A window is all that's there. The only thing we can do is jump.

Niamh Reid (13)
St Killian's College, Carnlough

Strange Events

Something scuttled under my skin. My mutant form was exposed again. I was in a mutant refugee camp in the heart of a desert. A group was sent to the city to try and make peace with the humans. Weeks passed and we ran out of food and water. With no water left, it was the end. We couldn't return to the city or we'd be killed immediately. Everyone lay sprawled out in the sun, dehydrated and too tired to move. Suddenly, the group reappeared on donkeys and exclaimed, "We did it!" But that was when the humans attacked.

Naoise McDonnell (12)

St Killian's College, Carnlough

The Crazy Chemicals

The last drop fell into the tube, however as it did, the test tube cracked and the dangerous acid leaked out. Gasps of fear could be heard around the room and many pupils were panic-stricken. Thankfully, the students were wearing their protective clothing. Nevertheless, it was necessary to quickly evacuate the class due to the risk of contamination. The teacher then carefully neutralised the acid with an alkaline solution and the classroom was closed until the hazard was dealt with and the room was cleaned and made safe again.

Zeke Hopkins (12)
St Killian's College, Carnlough

Monsters

I can't remember how it started but I'll try my best. The year was 3192. On my birthday, these blood-red monsters took over and ate my parents right in front of me and my brother. Ten years later, there is no one left, not that I know of. The outbreak started at my parents' lab. "Why do they eat you?" I hear you ask, well it's because that's how they turn you. I can still see them in my dreams, they attacked me. I cut off my arm...

Growl! I have to go now, they're coming...

Alanna Dewar (12)

St Killian's College, Carnlough

The Swan

Yet again, here we are on a cold subway train diverted over a mountain pass. Seemingly abandoned, precisely in the centre of the viaduct, the swans were closing in. Nineteen of us, freezing half to death. We had a 'Plan B' that was to die. The water was contaminated, the swans, they were like rabid dogs... The swans ate everyone. We had no food or water, there was hardly any to begin with, after all, I was only going from Trafalgar and Piccadilly. This was quite the detour. Every step we took led to disaster...

Thomas Irvine (13)
St Killian's College, Carnlough

The Walking Forest

A boy called James lived in a house beside a forest, but his parents told him never to go into the forest because it was dangerous. One day, he couldn't help himself and went in only to be bitten on the hand by a large, hairy spider. His hand started to swell and his skin started to peel off and he felt very sick. As days went past the boy died and everyone in the village got contaminated with the same disease and died. As the spiders took over the village the sign above read: *Contamination: Do not enter!*

Duncan McMullan (13)
St Killian's College, Carnlough

Duck Disease

One happy day, it was my birthday and I saw a duck. My friend Mick said, "I'll grab that and pet it, then everyone else can too!"
I saw the duck glowing, I said, "I'll pass."
Thirty minutes later, I thought, *Oh no!* as I saw Mick change. I ran for my life. I tripped and fell into a bunker. It was a lab. I saw the cure. Before I could grab it, I was touched, but I grabbed it and drank it! I went back to the park and put the cure in the water sprinklers and cured everyone!

Declan Higgins
St Killian's College, Carnlough

The Killer Bomb

It all started with a bomb, people were changing rapidly. People caught it by breathing, the disease spread in the air. When you were walking about, you could catch it like that and you turn into a zombie. Someone needed to find a cure for this dreadful disease or the whole world was in danger. Some of my friends were contaminated and were hunting me. I grabbed a shotgun but was afraid to pull the trigger because they were my friends. Help! I knew they were zombies but someone needed to find a cure.

Ben Erdis
St Killian's College, Carnlough

The Bug

I was creating a robot wolf. I went to get the bug but it was gone! If it got in the wrong hands, it could wipe out humanity. As I looked, I prayed that Dr Denis hadn't found it. He would turn it into a zombie disease! As I walked by a cleaner, the lights flashed on and off. I was shaking with fright, I started running. I heard a smash from Dr Denis' lab. I turned a corner and went in. There was a weird, green coloured liquid on the floor. I saw him. He didn't look the same...

Leanne Magill (12)
St Killian's College, Carnlough

Explosion

As the huge plume of smoke debris rose into the air, there was a mammoth wave of heat. Suddenly, the temperature fell and tiny particles of white dust drifted gently onto the barren land. It was strange. It was the middle of summer. Children ran out from their houses and began to catch the snow with their tongues in delight, as it was the first time they had been able to enjoy themselves since the first bomb. I soon came to my senses and remembered what I'd learned in school...

Oran McClintock (12)
St Killian's College, Carnlough

Everyone Dies

I tried to save them, they were covered in wretched spots and coughing blood. Me and my friend have got a cure for the plague. It's caused by diseased rats contaminating the water. Only the bottled water is pure, we have to filter and purify the water to help and give them a blue tablet to get rid of the sores. It worked for a while then something bad happened. Another break out happened... Everyone died, even me and my friend, the so-called saviours of the sick and weary.

Emily McAllister

St Killian's College, Carnlough

The Disease

Something scuttled under my skin. It was moving but no one could see. I went to see a doctor but there was nothing to see so I waited a week and went again. He told me it was an evil fly. He said I have got to have an operation or it could get infected. I skipped the operation and it got infected.
I turned into a giant monster. I wanted to eat people but no one was about. I found a little girl and swallowed her whole and an adult. We found a cure... lemon and honey!

Erin McGinley (12)
St Killian's College, Carnlough

The Bomb

The bomb had hit New York. Mysterious planes flew over the city at night. The TV turned on. "The city has gone into chaos after the news about this bomb," said the newsreader. The effects of this were very noticeable. Hair fell out and red spots showed up. Terrified toddlers were screaming, screaming like they'd seen a monster. When you saw the signs, you knew you only had six hours to live. Scientists were doing all they could, but it wasn't enough.

Emily McNaughton (12)
St Killian's College, Carnlough

The Fortnite Zombie Apocalypse

When the storm came we hopped in the battle bus. I landed in Tilted. Someone got caught by the storm, they turned into a zombie. If anyone came into contact with them they would turn into a zombie. My friend Gilbert got caught, I was the only survivor. I found a cure for the zombies. I took it to my underground vault and I made more cures. I took my quad-crusher and splashed the cure at the zombies, then they all turned into humans and they were cured!

Damien James McKillop (12)
St Killian's College, Carnlough

The Deadly Daffodils

It was coming up to the end of winter and spring was on its way and I and my dad thought it was a nice day to go for a walk with the dog to see my mum's grave.

We went to my mum's grave and I saw these lovely daffodils. I picked some to put on mum's grave and I had one in my hand when the wind picked up and I felt my throat closing up. I screamed and fell to the ground.

I woke up in the hospital with a mask covering my face...

Ellie Hunter (13)
St Killian's College, Carnlough

The Slurry Zombie

Once upon a time on a cold, bad winter's day, a man called Willy Evans was spreading slurry on a field. Then a well-known mountain climber came to talk to Willy. Slurry got in the mountain climber's mouth and he turned into a zombie. He went around killing everybody on Earth but one. Big Alistar Packer got his rifle and killed the zombie and everybody came back to life and big Alistar Packer was a hero in the end.

Neil McLaughlin (13)
St Killian's College, Carnlough

The Contamination Snake

Lucy was out walking, she heard splashing and rustling noises coming from the drain. She looked down, out slithered a snake and it bit her leg. She rushed home to tell her parents, feeling very unwell. There had been talk about dangerous snakes on the news and now Lucy was scared. The only cure was to find the snake with a special pattern. Do you think she'll find it...?

Ellie McDonnell (13)
St Killian's College, Carnlough

Zombie Apocalypse

For months now, scientists have been trying to create a formula that changes people into zombies. The scientists were experimenting on a fly that can spread the virus, but the fly escaped from the lab. The fly had bitten everyone in the city, turning them into zombies with green glowing eyes. The city was deserted with only zombies looking for survivors.

Oisin Toal (12)
St Killian's College, Carnlough

The Hali Virus

It all happened so fast, it was like wildfire spreading, infecting all those who were healthy and came into contact with this plague. The worst part of it all was having to watch your loved ones become horrific monsters and attempt to devour you like a beast chowing down on its prey. The infection starts by slurring your works and then eventually turns your eyes blood-soaked red and gave you a malnourished look. Eventually, it spreads to the brain and kills you. The mouths of the infected hang open like swings and their bodies are drenched in blood.

Niall Gary Morrell (14)
St Mary's Christian Brothers' Grammar School, Belfast

The End Of The World

It all started with mutated chickens that were put into chicken boxes. Anyone who ate one turned into a zombie and that was how it all started. Everyone except me and my family died. But in the end, we all died and the world became overpopulated with zombies. They combined all countries of the world into one and reigned and produced baby zombies but then realised they had nothing to eat. They went into the shops left by humans and stole food or ate their young. That was how the world ended.

Alyssa Campbell (12)
St Mary's College, Londonderry

The Wipeout

The huge, metal door screeched open. The catastrophe had struck the world. The survivors stared, mouths gaping at the horrible wasteland in front of them. About twenty men had searched for others. The underground bunker held up for almost five years but supplies were running low. Hundreds of burnt up bodies lay before them. Suddenly, a cry for help called. It was coming toward them through the thick, smoky air. The last explorers crawled toward them, dragging an empty bag. "Monsters, they're coming! We have to go!" he screamed. He was delirious and the only monsters were the humans.

Tomas Doyle
St Mary's Grammar School, Magherafelt

The End Of The World

"The disease spread, killing its victims within a day," said the startled man to his therapist. "The blood-curdling screams still echo through my mind. One day, the young man next door is healthy, the next he's gone."

"And how did this... change you, as you worked as a doctor desperate to save lives, but you couldn't?" questioned the therapist.

The man replied, "It feels like hell, just to know that there are people out there dying kills me inside. If we can't find a cure soon, our kind will come to a sudden end!"

Aodhan James Heaney (12)

St Mary's Grammar School, Magherafelt

Zombie Contamination

Scientists in Texas thought they finally had a cure for cancer, all they had to do was one last test to make sure and then... suddenly, their great rivals burst through the doors with guns. They wanted the cure but the Texan scientists would not give it to them. So their rivals tried to shoot poisoned darts at them but they missed and it went into the cure! The scientist suddenly dropped the glass. It was contaminated... It was quickly spreading along the room. Everyone was dying and changing into alien-like zombie monsters, trying to eat each other's brains...

Caroline O'Kane
St Mary's Grammar School, Magherafelt

The Blood

The disease was spreading by the minute, everyone itches within an inch of their lives, they're ready for their lives to be over. Doctors, scientists, even witches tried their best to cure 'The Blood'. I bet you're wondering how this awful disease came on to this Earth. Well, let me take you back in time, in 1953 Doctor Ringer released a horrible toxic liquid into the pipes of New York. Thirteen years later, a plumber was working on an old house that was being renovated when he burst a pipe and the horrible toxic liquid exploded over New York...

Anna Hurl (12)
St Mary's Grammar School, Magherafelt

Cough Cough

The thin green mist moved like a toxic veil in the sky, entrapping the horizon. Cal stumbled over the rubble, his home now a wreck. *Cough, cough.* His blood and saliva spewed onto his rag, it had been turned a dark scarlet from his blood... and the previous owner's.

His plan was to find food then to wait the storm out. The gas was highly volatile, even the slightest spark would blow up a street. He thought back to that night, but quickly regained his focus; his thoughts wouldn't bring them back. All he could do now was walk.

Patrick Kevin Glackin (12)
St Mary's Grammar School, Magherafelt

The Mutation

I'll never forget 16th February 2013. With only fifteen humans left on Earth, we had to fight for our lives against this humungous flesh-eating monster that had already devoured the rest of the world. As the monster and I stood face to face, I suddenly remembered the story that we did in school about David and Goliath. I grabbed my sling and with all my strength, I pulled back the stone and, with great aim and precision, I got him right between the eyes. I watched as the monster swayed round and round and fell with a tremendous thud!

Nicholas Cleary (12)
St Mary's Grammar School, Magherafelt

The Noodles Infection

I was mind-blown when I heard that my favourite snack was now a deadly infection. It was 2039 and the noodle infection was starting to kick in, people were sleeping on the streets with giant purple spots on their foreheads, though it had spread down their necks and arms. I was always sick, worried if I would catch the disease. Every Monday, I would visit the hospitals and talk to the patients. I knew it really helped to have someone to talk to. Two years later, the noodles disease is still an illness though it can be dealt with.

Conn McAllister (12)
St Mary's Grammar School, Magherafelt

The Last Of Us

A horrifying disease has killed 99% of Earth's population. No one knows what caused it but a small group of scientists are close to finding a cure. Dr Collins has been going crazy recently, he's been in his room praying for the past few days. I don't know if he is infected or not. I need to watch him carefully. The next day, I went to his room and he was gone and everyone else was dead. All of a sudden, *bang!* I got hit in the back of the head, "I guess his is my end too!"

Michael Mooney (12)
St Mary's Grammar School, Magherafelt

Locked

We sat at the cracked window, pale, hungry and staring out at the darkening sun. It was coming... the nights are always the worst. I sat shaking, wondering as I looked around at the people left in this cramped, smelly, damp room; who would be missing in the morning? Then a blood-curdling scream that went on for ages came from the corner. I saw her tiny frail body being ripped from the floor. It had come, it was hungry, one eye stared at me as it fed viciously and threw the carcass at me! I'm next!

Caitlin Craig (11)

St Mary's Grammar School, Magherafelt

Miracle

There they were on the big, white moon. Just Peter and his son Tiernan and their dog Flufster. They had left their home and gone to the moon. They were being chased by aliens all over the moon. They ran and they ran, trying to get away from the aliens but it was no use, the aliens were behind them the whole time. Then they wished for a miracle to happen. Flufster the dog wagged her tail and *zap, flash!* They had landed home safe and sound. Well... they were alright but everyone else was gone.

Dearbhla Quinn (12)
St Mary's Grammar School, Magherafelt

Last Man Standing

It was the middle of the night when he heard shrieks of horror. He got out of bed, looked out the window and saw a fog covering the ground. He looked around the city and spotted a woman putting out the washing, the fog approached her. When she breathed it in, she collapsed, then her head popped up with red spots all over her body. Her dark, dead eyes blended into the darkness. He lived on the highest floor of the highest building. It broke in through the window, he was the last man standing.

Ultan Tomas Mallon (12)
St Mary's Grammar School, Magherafelt

The Creatures Of The Night

We were shut off from the outside world. Two years ago, an act of paranormal struck this very nation, people started to wander around in the night, creeping on people, biting their necks. We were plagued with vampires. I opened the door and stepped into the sunlight.

There were seven of us, that we knew, who'd survived what we called The Great Contamination. Others were ambushed in the middle of the night, bitten and their blood sucked from their veins, replaced with the vampire DNA.

I entered an unnaturally quiet, dark building and I felt two points upon my skin...

Cameron Newport Snell (14)

Torlands Academy, St Thomas

YOUNG WRITERS INFORMATION

We hope you have enjoyed reading this book – and that you will continue to in the coming years.

If you're a young writer who enjoys reading and creative writing, or the parent of an enthusiastic poet or story writer, do visit our website **www.youngwriters.co.uk**. Here you will find free competitions, workshops and games, as well as recommended reads, a poetry glossary and our blog.

If you would like to order further copies of this book, or any of our other titles, then please give us a call or order via your online account.

Young Writers
Remus House
Coltsfoot Drive
Peterborough
PE2 9BF
(01733) 890066
info@youngwriters.co.uk

Join in the conversation!

 YoungWritersUK    @YoungWritersCW